A LAST HOPE NOVEL

J. S. SCOTT

Inevitable

Copyright © 2025 by J. S. Scott

All rights reserved. No part of this document may be reproduced or transmitted in any form or by any means, electronic, mechanical, photocopying, recording, or otherwise, without prior written permission.

Proof editing by Virginia Tesi Carey
Cover designed by Sarah Kil Creative

ISBN: 979-8-269268-08-8 (Print)
ISBN: 978-1-959932-36-9 (E-Book)

CONTENTS

Prologue.. 1
Chapter 1... 5
Chapter 2... 12
Chapter 3... 19
Chapter 4... 25
Chapter 5... 31
Chapter 6... 38
Chapter 7... 45
Chapter 8... 51
Chapter 9... 57
Chapter 10.. 64
Chapter 11.. 71
Chapter 12.. 77
Chapter 13.. 85
Chapter 14.. 92
Chapter 15.. 99
Chapter 16.. 107
Chapter 17.. 115
Chapter 18.. 121
Chapter 19.. 129
Chapter 20.. 135

Chapter 21	143
Chapter 22	151
Chapter 23	157
Chapter 24	163
Chapter 25	169
Chapter 26	175
Chapter 27	183
Chapter 28	189
Chapter 29	195
Chapter 30	201
Chapter 31	207
Chapter 32	213
Epilogue	219

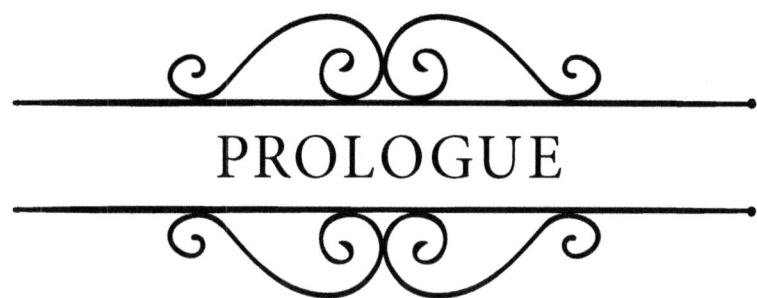

PROLOGUE

Marshall
Virginia Beach, Virginia
Fourteen Years Earlier...

It was time for me to go.

I'd been telling myself the same thing over and over for the last forty-five minutes. I'd stalled around by taking a long shower in the master bath while the beautiful, blonde female sleeping in the bed was oblivious and sleeping like an angel.

It had been a long night for us because we knew it was our last night together.

Emma.

What in the hell had I been doing with an extraordinary woman like her for the last five days?

And why in the fuck was I having such a hard time leaving when I'd known from day one that this was just a brief fling for both of us?

Neither of us had wanted any commitments or strings attached to the time we'd spent here together in Virginia Beach.

She'd said she was on vacation, and I wasn't looking for a relationship.

I was *never* looking for a relationship.

I certainly hadn't planned on hooking up with anyone, either.

I'd just finished a really rough mission as the commander of a SEAL team, and all I'd wanted during my leave was to temporarily put that operation out of my mind.

I hadn't planned on actually succeeding at that goal.

I *never* did.

My thoughts were never far away from my job. My career in the military was my entire life, and I'd made that choice very willingly a long time ago.

However, for just a short time, I'd actually let a woman get to me.

I had managed to put that recent mission out of my mind for a while because I'd been totally distracted by *her*.

Emma.

I wasn't sure how she'd managed to get under my skin, but she had.

Five days!

We'd only been together for five fucking days, and now I was dragging my feet about leaving her.

Emma and I had literally bumped into each other.

Okay, maybe that wasn't *exactly* the truth.

I'd practically mowed her over while she was window shopping in town because my thoughts were consumed with my previous operation at the time.

I'd stopped to help her up.

It *was* my fault she fell to the ground in the first place.

And then...I'd done something totally out of character once I'd looked into the prettiest pair of blue eyes I'd ever seen. I'd invited her to get a drink to apologize.

Hell, I shouldn't have done that.

I never did things like that.

But for some unknown reason, I had, and she'd actually accepted, even though I'd expected her to politely decline.

She was gorgeous and extremely young to be going out for a drink with a cantankerous, grumpy guy like me.

The days that followed were like something out of a fantasy.

Emma was no pushover.

She was fearless, and she'd pried me out of my shell like no woman ever had before.

Most women—hell, most people in general—treated me with a healthy amount of respect because I was a humorless, introverted, large man with an attitude.

I still wasn't sure what Emma saw in me that she actually liked.

I *wasn't* a likable guy, but the connection and attraction between the two of us was definitely mutual.

We'd agreed not to share any personal information, and no promises.

Strangely, we'd found plenty to talk about anyway.

I might not know her last name, where she came from, or what she did for a living, but I knew her likes and dislikes.

I also knew every beautiful curve of her body.

Her scent.

Her taste.

Dammit! Those things would *definitely* haunt me once I'd left this beachfront home.

I shook myself out of my musings.

Certainly, I'd forget about her as soon as I was back on base and researching our next mission.

There was no space in my brain for anything else.

Never had been and never would be.

The time I'd spent with Emma had simply been a brief reprieve from my normal life.

It *had* to be that way.

There was no room in my life for a romantic relationship, and I'd always been okay with that.

Most special forces guys had a hard time maintaining any kind of romantic relationship.

Personally, I'd never even tried to do it myself.

I'd seen too many relationships fail in my occupation, and I had absolutely nothing to offer a woman.

I was an asshole with no joy in my life. No woman deserved a man like me.

Especially Emma...

She deserved someone who would treat her right someday. A guy who could make time for her.

I finally picked up my duffle bag from the floor and walked to the side of the bed.

The thick layer of ice around my heart cracked just a little as I glanced down at the serene expression on her face as she slept.

Yeah, unfortunately, I'd remember *her*.

The memories over the last several days played over and over in my head as my eyes swept over her beautiful face.

Christ! I needed to get out of Emma's vacation rental because I was actually tempted to leave her my number, even though we'd promised each other this was all just a fling.

Leave, Marshall. Get your ass moving.

Leaving my number so we could stay in contact was *not* part of the deal I'd made with Emma, and I was a man of my word.

I dropped a small box onto the bedside table next to her side of the bed before I turned and walked toward the door.

Gifts were probably not part of the deal, either, but I didn't give a shit.

Maybe there was part of me that wanted Emma to remember the last five days because I knew I'd probably never entirely manage to forget them.

Hell, they'd been the best five days of my life.

Move, Marshall. You're married to the Navy and always will be.

I was close to forty years old.

My life was already mapped out with nothing but the SEALS in my future.

I was too damn old to change, and Emma was way too good for a guy like me.

I opened the front door, then flipped the lock on the handle so the door would lock behind me.

I took the stairs quickly, trying to put some distance between myself and temptation.

I definitely wouldn't change, but for the first time in my life, there had been a woman in my life that had made me temporarily wish that I could.

CHAPTER 1

Marshall
San Diego, California
The Present...

"Here's your damn cookies that Shelby made for you," Wyatt Durand grumbled unhappily as he reluctantly dropped the tin of cookies onto the table as he entered the conference room at Last Hope headquarters.

I was already seated in front of a laptop computer at the long table. I smirked as I snagged the cookies and put them near my computer.

Wyatt was possessive about his wife's cookies, and he hated it when she gave them to anyone else but him.

I liked him, but I enjoyed harassing him about Shelby. It wasn't that long ago when he'd sworn he wasn't interested in any kind of commitment or relationship.

"Was it really that painful?" I asked Wyatt with a straight face.

"Yes," he answered gruffly as he took a seat next to me in the room. "Shelby is a chef, but she doesn't bake that often. I like you, Marshall, but I'd prefer to keep her baked goods for myself."

Wyatt was a billionaire and perfectly capable of flying in the best pastries on the planet to his home in San Diego.

Not that Shelby's cookies weren't incredible. I coveted them myself. I was pretty sure that Wyatt was possessive of *anything* that was created by his wife.

I was also certain that Wyatt hated it when Shelby did something nice for another guy, and she did plenty of nice things for me. She thought I was a lonely, older bachelor who didn't take good care of myself on my own.

She was partially right.

I wasn't lonely, and even though I was twelve years older than her husband, Wyatt, I wasn't ready to think of myself as truly old. However, I was a fifty-three-year-old man who was obsessed with my job and my private volunteer rescue organization that we called Last Hope. Shelby *was* probably right about me not paying much attention to my personal well-being most of the time.

I was too obsessed with our hostage rescues to think about what I ate or cooking for myself most of the time.

Wyatt and I were currently sitting at Last Hope headquarters in San Diego, a high-tech facility with impenetrable security.

We monitored and ran our rescue missions from these headquarters while one of our volunteer teams rescued hostages in the field.

Every one of the men on our teams were previous special forces.

Mostly, we took on cases that couldn't or wouldn't be handled by the government.

I'd founded the organization after I'd been forced to retire as a SEAL commander because of an injury to my leg that had left me with my leg still intact. *Barely.* I had a noticeable limp, and I hadn't been able to return to my duties in the military.

What had started off as a small volunteer rescue operation to fill a gap in the system had morphed into a covert, international organization over the years.

The funding from five billionaires who had signed on to volunteer a few years after the creation of Last Hope, including Wyatt, had boosted Last Hope to another level.

Not only did I have amazing funding for a high-tech operation, but the skills those men provided to help me run complex operations from our operation room here were invaluable. All five of them were top-notch previous special forces.

I took a sip of the strong coffee I'd brewed in the kitchen and swallowed before I asked, "Exactly why are we here right now? I know Brock and Nate requested a conference call immediately, but why the urgency?"

Brock and Nate were half of a very important volunteer team based in Michigan. Although we had previous special forces volunteers scattered across the globe, they were the A-team we called on the most for hostage rescues. They'd been part of Wyatt's Delta Force team for years, and they'd never had a failed operation as long as they'd been volunteering for Last Hope.

Wyatt shrugged. "I don't have any more information than you do," he informed me. "But if they say it's an emergency, I'm not going to argue. They never ask us for anything for all of the things they do for Last Hope, and they're still part of my team even though we aren't serving in Delta together anymore."

I nodded sharply. "Agreed. If they have a problem, I'm here to help them resolve it."

My fingers flew across the keyboard of the laptop and logged us into the meeting to wait for Brock and Nate to join us.

If Brock and Nate needed information, I was the guy to hit up.

I'd formed an intricate network of informants and useful people to know on both sides of the law throughout my years as a SEAL commander. I'd added even more to that list after my years in the military were over through Last Hope and my contract job with the government.

I was also one of the best hackers on the planet, and there was very little information I couldn't obtain if I needed it. There was no conceit about my skills. They were simply...a fact.

Having a genius IQ had come in handy over the years, and the areas where I was especially gifted were technology, gathering intel, and an uncanny ability to recall almost any fact or information I'd learned in the past.

I watched my screen as Brock dropped into the meeting and his face appeared on the screen.

I didn't know our Michigan team as well as Wyatt did, but I could tell that the younger man was stressed.

And it was damn hard to stress out a previous Delta Force operative.

Brock, Nate, Gage, and Seth were around Wyatt's age, and they all had balls of steel.

I nodded at Brock. "Wyatt is here with me. What's your situation?" I asked abruptly.

I wasn't known for being a warm and fuzzy kind of guy.

I cut right to the point.

Brock actually looked relieved that I didn't bother to make idle conversation.

"Nate's here, too," he answered as Nate's face popped onto the screen. "We have a friend that's missing. She left four days ago for a consulting job in Lania with Prince Niklaus. I told her to check in with me every morning. Lania might be considered a safe country now, but it was a hellhole not that many years ago. I heard from her the first and second day, but she missed her check-in yesterday, and I haven't heard from her this morning, either. She's not answering texts or calls from anyone."

Fuck! I hated Lania. Most people who were previous special forces still did, even though it was considered a tourist mecca these days. The country was in the middle of the Mediterranean Sea with pristine beaches and white sand beaches, which the tourists loved. To me though, it would always be a country that I'd taken way too many hellish trips to when it was a war-torn, small island nation consumed in civil war.

Back then, the rebels had taken hostages, and few of them had lived to tell their stories.

Even after the rebels had supposedly been eradicated, two women had been taken hostage by a few straggling rebels who had remained hidden on the desolate side of the island. Those women were now the wives of two of my billionaire partners who helped to run Last Hope.

Thank fuck we'd actually managed to rescue those two geologists who had been there for geological exploration.

I'd hoped to hell that I'd seen the last of Lanian rebels and Lania.

"What's the concern?" I asked Brock abruptly. "Prince Nick assured me that all of the rebels were long gone and that Lania was a safe tourist destination now."

I'd made it a point to become acquainted with Prince Nick a long time ago, and we still kept in touch.

"The rebels are gone," Nate agreed. "But the king isn't well physically now. There are a few political enemies who aren't thrilled about the possibility of Prince Nick becoming the king. Some of them are resistant to the changes he's made."

Prince Nick of Lania was unofficially the reigning monarch because his father, the king, had become too demented to make decisions for his country.

I knew the modernization of his country hadn't been popular with everyone, especially those who didn't want to see the country become a true democracy in the future.

"We can't get verification on this," Brock added. "But we heard from confidential sources that there was an assassination attempt on Prince Nick. We know that you have contacts in Lania, and that you know Prince Nick. We need information, Marshall."

"I'll contact him," I assured Brock. "What kind of work was this woman doing in Lania?"

"She's a marketing designer," he replied. "She's been working with Nick for a while now to improve Lania's brand. He wants the world to see Lania as a safe, beautiful, and prosperous country after years of war. Their economy is growing fast from tourism."

"Maybe she just got busy," I suggested.

Brock shook his head. "No. She's not like that. If she makes a promise, she keeps it. She knows we'd all be worried if she didn't check in with us. Something isn't right. I can feel it."

"Are we talking about Emma?" Wyatt asked grimly.

Brock nodded. "Yeah. You met her when you visited here, Wyatt. You know her well enough to realize that she'd never just ignore checking in."

"Yeah, I agree," Wyatt replied, his voice concerned. "She's definitely not a flake."

"When is this woman due back?" I questioned.

"In a week," Nate said gruffly. "We can't wait that long. If Emma is in trouble, we need to find out now. We were hoping that you could help us get some intel, Marshall."

"You really think this woman is in trouble?" I asked Brock with a frown. "We don't even know if this assassination attempt is real, and what would anyone achieve by kidnapping an American woman?"

Really, the woman could be anywhere.

Maybe she was in Lania for work, but it did have amazing beaches and other things to do for leisure.

Maybe this female wanted a break and didn't want to be found for a few days.

However, I couldn't deny the fact that Brock's gut instinct was always spot on.

"The kidnapping of an American could kill their tourist growth," Brock mused. "Or maybe they just want her as leverage because she was with Nick."

I supposed either of those things could be motives if someone really wanted to hurt Nick.

"I'm going to need all of the data you have on this woman," I said. "Photos, license, and passport info if you have it."

"Brock and I are getting ready to leave for Lania. I already sent all the info I have to your email," Nate answered grimly. "We'd just like to get as much information as possible before we leave."

That didn't surprise me. If this woman was important to them, they were going to go after her. Whether she was in trouble…or not.

Wyatt pulled his phone out of his pocket. "I have a few photos of Emma that I took the last time I was visiting in Cherry Cove."

He enlarged a photo and turned his phone around so I could see it.

My heart nearly stopped as I glanced at the picture of a beautiful, blonde woman manning a barbecue grill with a water view in the background.

The smile on her face and the mischief in those ocean blue eyes as she looked at the camera were unmistakable.

Fuck! Emma was a common name. I'd never dreamed that we were discussing a woman I'd known intimately a long time ago.

Maybe it had been fourteen years since I'd seen her face, but it *was* Emma.

The woman I'd never forgotten, no matter how hard I'd tried over the years.

"Hold off on leaving for Lania," I said hoarsely. "I'll hop the first plane I can get to Cherry Cove after I get the intel you need. I'll be in touch tonight."

CHAPTER 2

Marshall

"Tell me what's going on, Marshall," Wyatt insisted after we'd wrapped up the video conference with Brock and Nate. I closed my laptop after logging out of the meeting room. "I'm not sure what you're asking," I said innocently, but my mind was racing with all of the things I needed to do.

I grabbed my laptop and started to get up, but Wyatt put a strong hand on my shoulder to keep me from standing as he grumbled, "We've known each other for years, Marshall. I respect you, and I've always respected your privacy. But I would like to think that we're friends. You don't leave San Diego because you always want to be near the headquarters in case something comes up. And you sure as hell don't volunteer to go out of state to find a missing person. It's completely out of character for you, and I want to know why you're doing it now. Something about this situation is personal for you. It would have to be to get you away from headquarters. I get that you don't share much personal information about yourself with anyone, but I have to call bullshit on this one. I am your friend, whether you want that friendship or not. Level with me this time, Marshall. You helped me when

Shelby's life was in danger. I'd like to help you. Hell, you know every single one of us would help if you'd let us."

It wasn't that I didn't trust my partners with anything personal. Truth was, I didn't have a personal life to speak about.

I worked as a contractor for the federal government, which *nobody* knew because most of my intel work involved black ops. I didn't talk about that job, but I had a feeling that they all suspected that I had some pretty high connections within the federal government for some reason.

All of my spare time was dedicated to Last Hope and our operations here.

I lived and breathed intel and technology almost every waking hour of my day, which made me a pretty boring, reclusive kind of guy.

Hell, I probably owed Wyatt the truth about Emma, even though the brief fling had happened a long time ago.

He and the four other billionaires who helped Last Hope operate at its current level were the closest things I had to friends.

Wyatt was probably the most like me, which is why we understood each other so well.

Before he'd met Shelby, he'd been almost as reclusive and standoffish as I was now.

Wyatt would also end up being in charge of Last Hope headquarters operations while I was gone, so I probably did owe him some kind of explanation.

There were no hostage rescues brewing at the moment, but things could pop up in a hurry.

"What do you know about Emma?" I asked grudgingly. "And how exactly is she connected to our Michigan team?"

I'd spent five incredible days with her, but I didn't even know her last name, much less anything about her current life.

He lifted a brow. "Why do you want to know about her personal life?"

Dammit! How could I tell him that I needed to know that she wasn't the love interest of one of the men on our Michigan team or that I wanted to know everything about her now that I knew exactly where she was located?

That was just out of curiosity, of course.

My need to know wasn't exactly *personal*.

Honestly, it shouldn't matter if she was involved with one of the guys from the Michigan team.

Emma and I hadn't seen each other for almost fourteen years.

However, I'd wondered about Emma for years, and it was probably time for me to get some answers.

If her disappearance was going to involve Last Hope, it was critical that I find out as much as possible about her, right?

"I know her, Wyatt," I finally admitted gruffly. "We met fourteen years ago in Virginia Beach while I was still on active duty. We spent five days together there while I was on leave. We agreed to keep things simple and enjoy those five days together without sharing a lot of personal information about ourselves. I don't even know her last name, but those were probably the best days of my life. I was injured not long after on a mission. If I hadn't gotten injured, I might have tried to track her ass down, although it would have been difficult since I knew almost no personal information about her. It didn't take me more than a few hours to realize I should have left her my contact information, but by that time, she was already gone. She left the same day I did to return to wherever she called home."

Wyatt's eyebrows rose in surprise as he replied, "Whoa! Okay, I have to admit, I didn't see that one coming. You…and Emma? That just seems so…so…"

Since Wyatt didn't seem to know what to say that wasn't insulting to me, I finished for him drily, "Unlikely? Yeah, I know. I didn't exactly know her age, but I knew she was a lot younger than I was. She was also a lot nicer and more personable. I never understood why she was attracted to a grumpy, older guy like me. We were total opposites, but maybe that was why I was attracted to her. I'm also not the same guy I was back then. I can't say I was a pleasant man when I was a SEAL commander, but I wasn't the complete asshole I am now."

Wyatt shook his head. "You've dedicated your entire life to helping innocent people, Marshall. You are not an asshole. I guess it just surprised me that you and Emma were together at one time. But I see the attraction. She's an amazing woman, and it's hard to be pessimistic whenever she's around. I don't know her that well, but she's really close to the team in Michigan. She's like a sister to all of them. They've all been close for years. I know that her full name is Emma Lockwood, and I remember Brock mentioning that she was forty-five, so you're definitely not old enough to be her daddy. She still looks young for her age. I guess she did back then, too."

Had she really been over thirty when we were together in Virginia Beach? She was eight years younger than me, but back then, she'd looked like she was in her early twenties. She'd looked…really young. Wyatt was right. She still looked young judging by the photo I'd seen.

"Does she know they operate for Last Hope?" I asked curiously.

"Nope," Wyatt replied firmly. "You know everyone involved in Last Hope keeps it under wraps except for their significant other who almost has to know because our guys take off at a moment's notice. It drives Emma crazy when they just disappear and reappear like ghosts, but they've never explained exactly what they do when they have to go. They trust her, but Last Hope is a very covert operation, and the team has never shared that information with anyone. They were Delta. They're used to keeping secrets. So, are you hoping to rekindle that old romance with Emma? Is that why you want to go check on her safety yourself?"

If Wyatt was asking that question, Emma obviously wasn't involved in a committed relationship.

I hated myself for being so damned relieved that she was single.

Really, what did it matter now if she was married or single?

That brief fling had happened a long time ago, and I wasn't the same man I'd been before that mission that had nearly taken my leg.

I didn't want to rekindle anything with Emma.

I wasn't married to the military anymore, but I lived for my job and Last Hope now.

I was probably just concerned because I'd once known her personally and spent the happiest days of my life with her a very long time ago.

"Hell, no," I grunted as I sent Wyatt a look of disbelief. "She's young, and she's still just as beautiful as she was fourteen years ago. Do you really think she'd want to rekindle a romance with a lame, old guy like me? Maybe I'm just a little nostalgic. I'd like to see for myself that she's safe."

Wyatt snorted. "You're not a lame, old guy. I have a feeling you could kick my ass if you really wanted to, and I'm twelve years younger than you are. You keep yourself in shape." He paused thoughtfully before he added, "I'll get my private jet ready. It can get you to Cherry Cove quickly, and it might be needed to fly to Lania."

I did keep in shape, but I was still lame with a gimpy leg. It was second nature for me to keep my body in shape after so many years in the military. I couldn't run anymore, but I worked out at home and swam hard in my pool for aerobic exercise.

I also solo hiked whenever I had the time. I couldn't run, but I could walk for miles, even with my permanent limp.

It wasn't just my body that had changed. I'd changed over the years. I was probably even more jaded than I'd ever been as a SEAL Commander.

I was also a loner and pretty damn reclusive, and I liked it that way.

I nodded my thanks to Wyatt. "The jet would be helpful."

"I'll handle it," he said as he texted what I presumed was his flight crew. "All you have to do is get to the airport."

"Do you really think Emma could be in some kind of trouble?" I asked huskily.

My chest tightened. It had been years since I'd seen her, and our fling had happened in a different life for me. Still, the thought of her being alone and in trouble wasn't sitting well with me.

Wyatt shrugged. "I think it's possible. She's not a flake. If she promised to check in, she'd check in if she possibly could. She'd never ignore texts or calls. She'd never want any of the guys on the Michigan team to worry about her. I'm not sure what kind of trouble she could get into in Lania these days. Tons of tourists visit there every year, and there's been no issues. Although...none of *those* tourists are friends with Prince Nick. That concerns me a little. Are you sure you're ready to leave Last Hope headquarters? You probably see more of this place than your real home."

I grimaced. I was a control freak when it came to Last Hope, and it was rare for me not to be within driving distance of headquarters. "I'll live," I grumbled.

"You know you'll have a ton of volunteers to help if she's really missing," Wyatt reminded me. "I'd be going with you right now if Shelby wasn't suffering from morning sickness every morning. But if shit hits the fan, say the word and you'll have all the help you need. Judging by Brock's impatience, he's not going to wait long before he leaves to look for Emma."

Shelby was in the early stages of pregnancy, and I understood Wyatt's reluctance to leave her if it wasn't absolutely necessary. Although I'd probably never understand the desire to have a kid that all of my partners seemed to be going through right now.

"He needs to wait," I answered. "The Michigan team doesn't need to be flying blind without intel in Lania. We don't even know if she's really in trouble right now. How long before the jet is ready to go?"

Wyatt grinned. "It will be ready as soon as you get there. By the time you grab some stuff from your place, get some information, and get to the airport, they'll be ready to fly."

I considered myself a wealthy man from years of investing well, but I couldn't imagine having a private jet at my disposal.

Wyatt, Chase, Hudson, Jax, and Cooper lived in a world I couldn't even fathom.

All of them had been born into the world of the super-rich, and I admired the hell out of all of them because they'd chosen to give up that world for years to serve their country.

Hell, they were still serving their country as far as I was concerned. Last Hope was a priority for all of them, even though they had the funds to live in the lap of luxury without lifting a finger.

"Thanks," I said to Wyatt gratefully.

"Don't thank me," he insisted. "You're the one hauling your ass to Cherry Cove, and possibly Lania. I like her, Marshall, and if anyone can find her, it's you. I might be a billionaire, but I don't have your connections in high places."

"Hopefully I won't need any of them," I grumbled. "I'm hoping this is all just a misunderstanding."

My first priority was getting to Cherry Cove, but I was going to put in a call to Prince Nick before I left for the airport. I really needed to know if the rumored assassination attempt was true, and what the political situation looked like in Lania at the moment.

"Be careful," Wyatt said tersely as we moved toward the exit of the headquarters.

"I'm always careful," I shot back.

"Emma's a very intelligent woman," Wyatt informed me. "She wouldn't do anything risky. If she's in trouble, I guarantee it's not her fault. She mentioned that she did a double major at a college in Chicago in both marketing and graphic art. She also worked in the city for years as a marketing designer before she branched out on her own in Cherry Cove. She's built one hell of a reputation for herself in her field. She's not a naïve woman with no common sense."

I moved a little faster to get to the exit.

The more I learned about Emma, the more I was certain that she wasn't just lounging on the beach in Lania and ignoring her messages.

My gut instinct was telling me something was definitely not right, and even Wyatt's private jet probably couldn't get me to Michigan as quickly as I'd like.

CHAPTER 3

Emma

I was a woman who liked to keep things positive, but my optimism was starting to fade.

That probably wasn't unusual since I'd been chained to a metal support beam in a rundown building in a very desolate, wooded area of Lania for two days.

Nick and I had been visiting an unpopulated area on the Lanian coast that was slated for development in the future when that pleasant, beautiful day had turned into a nightmare.

Nick had wanted to give me some idea of what the area looked like, so I knew what I'd be working on for branding and marketing in the future.

We'd been flown in by helicopter, along with three bodyguards for Nick, something he hated but tolerated.

I'd been strolling the beach some distance from Nick when the bullets had started to fly.

I'd hit the sand after I'd recognized what was happening. Nick had been hauled bodily to the helicopter by his bodyguards as I'd been snatched up by the people responsible for the assassination attempt.

Nick had tried to get to me, but he'd been no match for his three, burly bodyguards whose only purpose was to protect the Crown Prince of Lania.

After that, my memories were somewhat blurry.

I'd fought the kidnappers, but they'd been way too powerful for one woman.

I'd been drugged to make me less combative and taken away to a wooded area of Lania that had probably been the home of the Lanian rebels at one time.

The cement building I was being held in looked like every other prison I'd seen for captives during the days of the Lanian rebellion.

It was dark except for one small, barred window. The place was also filthy, as if it hadn't been opened or used in years.

I couldn't move far from the metal post I was chained to right now.

I was thirsty as hell and lightheaded.

The only small amount of water I'd gotten was when they'd shoved another dose of drugs down my throat.

I knew I was getting seriously dehydrated, and I was feeling the effects of that dehydration.

And I had no idea how this ordeal was going to end.

Don't panic, Emma.

Having a meltdown wasn't going to help my situation.

I knew that Nick was turning Lania upside down to search for me. He'd been alive and screaming my name when he'd been shoved into that helicopter.

Nick had become a friend over the last few years and not just my client. I knew he'd keep searching for me until he found me.

I also knew that Brock, Nate, Gage, and Seth were eventually going to come looking for me, too.

I'd missed checking in with Brock both yesterday and today.

My friends had always been overprotective and watchful, even though I was older than all of them.

They were probably already looking for me.

My friends *would* find me.

I was really scared, but I had to stay hopeful.

I let out a tremulous sigh and tried to ignore the musty, rank smell of the prison and the fact that the building had probably been used for countless hostages in the past.

Hostages that had probably never left the building alive.

I had to keep reminding myself that I was apparently a political prisoner and not a rebel hostage, a woman Nick's enemies were probably using for leverage of some kind.

I'd been questioned excessively about my relationship with Nick and punched in the face over and over when I'd refused to answer their questions. I'd been punished for my lack of cooperation, but they weren't cutting off my fingers or body parts…yet.

Honestly, I didn't know *what* to tell them.

I was basically screwed.

If they thought I was a love interest to Nick, that could backfire.

If they knew we were nothing but friends and business associates that could get me killed because I wasn't that useful to them.

The kidnappers had insisted on knowing if I was Nick's secret girlfriend, but I'd remained stoic and quiet.

I'd decided it was better to stay silent.

Honestly, the idea of me being romantically attached to Nick was utterly ridiculous.

He was younger than me, and probably one of the most sought-after bachelors in the world.

We'd developed a really solid friendship over the years, but I'd definitely never been infatuated with the handsome prince.

Nick was…Nick.

He was a man who loved his country and wanted it to be a democracy.

He'd come a long way in achieving his goals of modernizing Lania, but as of now, the country was still ruled by the monarchy.

Lania was an old country that had been ruled the same way for centuries. Nick knew that change wasn't going to happen quickly.

Apparently, he had enemies that weren't on board with the changes that Lania was going through, and those changes would probably continue to happen even faster once Nick was king. He'd be the sole authority for Lania and not have to jump through hoops to make the current king's advisors happy.

I knew I wasn't in the hands of guerrilla rebels right now.

My guess was that the men who were holding me were the paid thugs of someone who was opposed to the changes in Lania and the fact that Nick would become king after his father's death.

I'd been beaten, deprived of food, and I'd gotten very little water.

However, if they'd been Lanian rebels, I probably would have been raped, brutalized, and killed by now.

Were these men capable of killing me?

I had no doubt that they were if they were instructed to off me by someone who was powerful in the Lanian government.

All four of my captors had the cold, calculated appearance of contract killers with no real emotion or empathy.

I shivered a little and lifted my hands to rub my upper arms that were littered with goosebumps.

I was terrified of my captors, but I couldn't let them see that fear.

I *had* to live through this.

Stop it, Emma! Get a grip. You are going to get through this.

I'd get rescued, and all of this would become a very bad memory.

I'd sleep in my own bed again in my little cottage in Cherry Cove.

God, I was exhausted, which was probably affecting my ability to keep those dark thoughts out of my head.

I'd dozed because of the drugs, but it was hard to truly sleep when I was propped up against a metal post. I was only shackled to the post by one wrist, but there was no way I was going to lie down on the filthy cement floor in this place. I'd already had a rat scamper across my leg. I wasn't putting my face on the ground. Luckily, I'd decided to dress in jeans and a T-shirt for my outing with Nick, so none of my bare skin was touching the cement, and I wanted to keep it that way.

I'd been over and over my options for two days.

Rescuing myself was impossible.

My shackles were heavy and secure.

Even if I could get loose by some miracle, the window was too small to escape through, and the door was metal-barred from the outside.

I heard that barrier slam into place every time one of my captors had closed the door.

Hoping for rescue from someone else didn't sit well with me, but it *was* my only option.

I wasn't used to asking for help from anyone.

However, I'd like nothing more than to see a bunch of muscular guys show up to break me out of this place right now.

I was extremely independent, but I wasn't stupid.

Some brawny show of strength was going to be needed to overtake the goons outside these walls.

Lania's military had improved enormously under Nick's rule, so there was some hope that I'd get my wish.

I just hoped it would happen sooner rather than later.

I was getting weaker from the drugs and lack of water and food.

I leaned my head against the post, closed my eyes, and tried to relax.

My hand went to the chain and pendant around my neck automatically, and I grasped it as I'd done many times in the past for comfort or strength.

I pulled the pendant out from its hiding place beneath my shirt so the assholes who were holding me didn't snatch it away like they had done with my cell phone and my purse.

The beautiful, antique necklace had been a gift I'd been given a long time ago by a man I'd never quite managed to completely forget.

It had been an outrageously expensive gift to a woman who was nothing more than a five-day fling to that guy.

Neither of us had wanted anything more than that fling, but it had always been hard for me to see those five days as something casual that meant nothing.

The gift was a necklace that I'd admired in a Virginia Beach antique shop when I was on vacation fourteen years ago.

I'd always loved antiques, especially anything art deco.

It was delicate for an art deco design, a simple circle encrusted with diamonds on a platinum chain.

I'd been forced to pass it up because of the price.

That special guy I'd been with had obviously noticed.

I'd found it on my bedside table when I'd woken up on that very last day in Virginia Beach.

I rarely took it off, and for some reason, holding that pendant gave me patience and strength when I'd needed it over the years.

Touching the beautiful circle had become an instinctive reaction for me when I was scared or uncertain.

I'd never really questioned why it helped me to touch the pendant, but it brought me a sense of calm that I really didn't understand.

Maybe it reminded me of the strong, powerful man who had given me the gift, or maybe it just reminded me of those incredible days I'd spent with him.

We hadn't stayed in touch.

That hadn't been part of the deal we'd made.

But I had cherished this gift from him ever since.

Fourteen years ago, I'd been going through a very rough time in my life.

Meeting someone like him, spending time with him, had been exactly what I'd needed at the time.

Most likely, he'd forgotten me a long time ago, but I'd definitely never forgotten him or what that encounter had meant to me.

I took a deep breath and let it out slowly.

I could feel my heart racing, and I wasn't sure whether it was caused by my dehydration or my fear that I'd die in this dark, musty place alone.

I clutched the circle so hard that it would probably leave an indent in my palm, but right now I needed all the help I could get.

CHAPTER 4

Marshall

"I'll go," Brock told me as we sat in the living room of his home in Cherry Cove. "Nate and I can handle this, Marshall."

Gage and Seth were currently on a trip in the Caribbean to help a friend who was opening a dive shop there.

Nate was occupied with checking all the gear they'd need for Lania.

I'd never been to Cherry Cove, and I'd only gotten a brief look at the town on my way from the airport in Traverse City.

The only things I'd really noticed were that it was on the coast of Lake Michigan and that it was a way smaller town than I was used to.

I shook my head. "Not happening. You and Nate are going to be needed to do the rescue."

"You realize your plan is absolutely insane," Brock mentioned from his seat in a recliner. "You're really going through with this? You're going to give yourself up to become a captive with Emma?"

I shrugged. "They want Prince Nick. That's not going to happen. They'll have to take me instead. He's going to convince them that I'm someone close to him that they can take instead of him…for now. Someone who can negotiate terms for his surrender."

It was total bullshit, but I was hoping they'd take the bait.

I continued, "Wyatt will track me from headquarters, get my location, and send you two in to recover both of us. It's the quickest way for us to get an exact location on Emma."

Conventionally searching for her could take a lot longer, and I highly doubted that they were bothering to feed her or give her the necessities. I also doubted that her captors had any intention of releasing her alive.

These enemies of Nick's were obviously going to try to hurt Nick in any way possible. Especially if they couldn't get to him themselves.

I'd discovered from Nick that the assassination attempt had been very real, and that Emma had been taken from a remote location in Lania that Nick and Emma had been visiting.

No doubt they were holding Emma for leverage because they could use her to get to Nick.

"I'm counting on you and Nate to get us out of there once Wyatt has a location," I told Brock.

Brock answered soberly, "You know we will, but what you're doing is risky, Marshall. And you've never been a leader who takes unnecessary risks. What's up with that? I think we can find Emma. I know you can do it without taking these risks."

I ran a frustrated hand through my hair. "Emma needs someone to be with her right now. I'm not willing to wait for days or weeks until we can locate her. You know that time is everything when it comes to hostages. This is the quickest option. I'm willing to take that risk to locate her."

To his credit, Nick had offered to trade himself for Emma, but that would be certain death for a prince whose country needed him.

I also knew Nick, and I didn't want to see him get dead.

I'd convinced him that his surrender would be certain death for both himself and Emma. There was no way in hell either of them would leave wherever they were holding her alive.

Nobody was going to die in this rescue mission.

It was already bad enough that they were holding Emma in fuck knew what conditions right now.

"Why?" Brock persisted. "It's not like you know and care about Emma like we do. Hell, I'm grateful for what you're doing. But I'm torn. I want Emma out of there as quickly as possible, but I don't like you putting your ass on the line for someone you don't even know."

"I do know her," I admitted. "We met fourteen years ago in Virginia Beach. I won't go into how we met or what we did there, but she's not a stranger to me. We haven't seen each other in fourteen years, but I'm not risking my life for someone I don't know."

I knew Brock well enough to know he wasn't going to let this go until he had an explanation and telling him the truth seemed to be my best option.

His eyes widened. "You and Emma were together?"

I lifted a brow. "I didn't say that we were together. I just said that I know her. Our acquaintance was brief. We spent some time together in Virginia Beach when I was active military."

"Then you already know that she's special," he commented. "She's like an older sister to us. Emma was the first one to befriend us here in Cherry Cove when we settled here after Delta, and we've all been like family ever since."

The woman *hadn't* been like a sister to me, but I did understand that Emma was special. "She has a way of getting under your skin," I told him.

Brock grinned. "And once that happens, she stays there. She tries to mother all of us, and she hates it that she usually can't. I kind of hate that our frequent disappearances worry her, but we've never told her about Last Hope."

"She's going to have to know now," I informed him.

There's no way that Brock and Nate could show up in Lania to rescue her without Emma knowing the truth.

"Honestly," Brock said. "It will kind of be a relief for her to know. You can trust her, Marshall. I don't know how well you two were acquainted, but she'd die before she'd let that secret out to anyone else. Especially if she knows that lives depend on her keeping that secret."

I nodded and checked my phone just like I'd been doing for the last fifteen minutes since I'd arrived at Brock's home.

I was waiting impatiently for a final confirmation from Nick that everything was a go.

"Did your time with Emma end on good terms?" Brock questioned.

I looked up at him. "Yeah. Why do you ask?"

He shrugged. "I guess I was hoping this would be a good surprise for Emma to see you and not a bad one. Obviously, you didn't stay in touch."

Talking about Emma had been difficult for me with Wyatt, and I'd worked closely with him for years.

There was no way I was completely spilling my guts to Brock.

I liked and respected the whole Michigan team, but our entire relationship had always revolved around Last Hope business.

I knew almost nothing about them personally.

I knew that Brock was a popular author of suspense novels in a fictional special forces world.

I'd read every one of those novels.

But that was the extent of my knowledge about his personal life.

"No hard feelings between the two of us," I said vaguely. "We knew the time we spent together would be brief. I was a SEAL commander, and she was a tourist on a short vacation."

"I don't suppose you want to expand on that explanation," Brock said drily.

"I don't," I told him. "I liked Emma and for some reason she seemed to like me. I'm not the same man I was back then, but I don't anticipate that she'll be unhappy to see me."

Brock held up a hand. "Okay, enough said. Just…take care of her, Marshall. She means a lot to all of us."

"That's my plan," I assured him.

"Has anyone ever told you that getting anything personal out of you is nearly impossible?" Brock questioned.

"I don't have a personal life," I said honestly. "My priority is and always will be Last Hope."

"It's kind of ironic that we've been working with you for years and never knew that you'd met Emma," Brock mused. "Wyatt has mentioned your name before when he was visiting here. She obviously didn't recall hearing that name before or she would have asked questions."

"She wouldn't," I said offhandedly as I glanced down at a text that had just come in from Nick. "She didn't know me as Marshall."

For some reason, that had been one of the rare times that I'd used my first name.

"Have you gotten word from Prince Nick that this crazy plan is a go?" Brock asked.

"Yeah," I confirmed as I finished reading the long text Nick had just sent. "His officials didn't give the kidnappers much of a choice if they want to talk about Nick giving himself up for Emma. They even cleared me to bring a pack with me. That's not negotiable. I want to make sure that Emma has water, food, and something to keep her warm at night. They can search it. They won't find anything."

My tracking device would be extremely tiny and undetectable, and the last place I'd put it was inside a backpack.

"I still think I should go in your place," Brock offered. "Gage and Seth are trying to get a flight back from the Caribbean as soon as possible. One of them could go with Nate. Marshall, it could be a long hike if they're really remote."

I shot Brock a scathing look. "Are you trying to say I'm too old and too lame to handle a long hike?"

He shook his head. "You don't really talk about what you're capable of doing when it comes to your leg. I know you're in shape. That's pretty obvious."

"I'm going. I'm capable of doing whatever needs to be done," I said gruffly. "If I didn't think I was up to the job, I'd let someone else do it. Emma's safety comes before anyone's ego. We can't count on Gage and Seth making it back before we need them. I'm flying tonight. I'm going to ask Jax to send his private jet here so it's on standby for you and Nate."

I couldn't really blame Brock for questioning my physical abilities. I did, in fact, have a limp. We very rarely saw each other in person, and I wasn't as close to the Michigan team as I was to Wyatt. We communicated a lot, but not ever about anything personal.

"That's all I need to know," Brock answered abruptly. "We won't be far behind you, Marshall. Wyatt will let us know once you're in place and we have your location."

Brock was all business now that we had a mission in process.

I could tell that he was still worried about Emma, but his training would keep that under wraps while he carried out this rescue.

We both stood.

"Do you need supplies?" Brock asked.

I shook my head. "The pack is ready and already on Wyatt's jet."

"I wish I had some peppermints for you to put in that pack. Emma doesn't eat a lot of sweets, but ice cream and peppermints are her weaknesses."

If I was the kind of man who ever smiled, I probably would have grinned at his comment. "The ice cream isn't going to happen," I told him. "But I have a bag of peppermints in the pack."

Maybe some things never changed.

Emma apparently had the same preferences as she'd had fourteen years ago.

Brock sent me a quizzical look. "You still remember a small detail like that from a short acquaintance all those years ago?"

"Photographic memory," I grumbled as I moved toward his front door.

There was nothing I didn't remember about Emma.

Her laugh.

Her smile.

Her voice.

Her smell.

Her taste.

Every single preference I'd discovered about her during our time in Virginia Beach felt like it was permanently imprinted in my brain.

Hell, photographic memory aside, there was no way I'd forget a single thing I'd learned about her.

Every single detail I knew about her had been haunting me for years.

CHAPTER 5

Emma

I'd decided that I could go a little longer without food, but I was so thirsty that my mouth felt as dry as a desert.

My head was pounding, and I wasn't as alert as I'd been on day one.

They hadn't bothered to force drugs down my throat today, so I hadn't even gotten that tiny sip of water today.

They probably assume that I'm so weak that I'm not going to fight them.

Honestly, I was weak. Lack of sleep and water were getting to me.

I was hungry, but I was a curvy woman. I wasn't exactly skin and bones from not eating.

However, I was on day three with very little water, and I was feeling it.

My brain didn't want to acknowledge that I could die in this filthy prison, but I was also realistic.

A person could only go three days without water before the internal organs started to shut down.

Don't give up, Emma.

There had to be tons of people looking for me.

As long as I was conscious, I could still be hopeful, right?

I'd been working hard to try to figure out a way to get the shackle around my wrist loose, but I didn't have a single tool to work with, and there wasn't even a tiny weakness in the solid steel.

I'd also gone through every link on the chain that was attached to that shackle. That sucker wasn't coming apart without tools to cut it.

I startled as I heard the heavy metal door open.

I hadn't seen my captors at all today, and my heart started to race.

We're they coming in to kill me because I wasn't useful to them?

God, I hated the fact that I couldn't seem to control my fear anymore.

My entire body tensed up as the door opened noisily.

I blinked as my eyes tried to adjust to being exposed to more light.

"We brought you some company," one of my captors said in heavily accented English.

Like me, the male figure I could make out had a shackle and chain attached to his left wrist, and he was pushed into the room with a force that propelled him toward the same support that held me prisoner.

I couldn't quite make out the man's facial features, and before I could take a better look after my vision cleared, the man was behind me. I could hear him being attached to the same support beam that I was.

A moment later, the door was closed and locked.

"Emma? Are you okay?" the man asked as he dropped to the ground beside me.

Oh, God.

That voice.

I knew it, and it certainly wasn't Nick or some random stranger.

"Colin?" I said weakly.

The tiny window gave me very little light, but I could see the large outline of the body sitting next to me.

I couldn't see any of his facial details, but his voice sounded exactly the same.

I wondered for a moment if I was hallucinating in my dehydrated state.

How was it possible that the man I'd spent time with fourteen years ago in Virginia Beach was *here*.

In Lania.

And now being held captive with me.

"It's me," he confirmed abruptly. "Are you okay? I didn't get a very long look at you, but it looks like your face is bruised."

"I-I'm fine," I stuttered, still stunned that Colin was really here.

What in the world was he doing *here*?

"I've got water," he said gruffly as he appeared to dig into some kind of pack that he'd brought with him into the prison. "Have they been giving you food and water?"

"Neither one," I told him breathlessly. "I think I'm pretty dehydrated."

"Fuck!" he said, his voice irritated as he handed me a bottle. "Drink slowly. One sip at a time. I have plenty, but you can't have that much water hitting your system at the same time. It will probably come right back up if you do."

I wanted to guzzle the water as fast as I could, but I did as he instructed.

I closed my eyes with gratitude as I slowly quenched my thirst.

"How is it possible that you're here?" I said between sips. "Did they kidnap you, too?"

"No," he answered as he pulled more stuff from that pack. "When I heard that you'd been kidnapped, I came here willingly. They think I'm here to negotiate Prince Nick's surrender. They weren't going to refuse having another friend of Nick's for leverage. I'm getting you the fuck out of here, Emma."

"You and Nick are friends?" I questioned, still confused.

I hadn't talked to Colin in fourteen years, and I was still more than a little stunned to meet up with him again.

I'd honestly thought I'd never see him again.

"More of an acquaintance," he clarified. "But they don't know that. I brought food for you, but we better let that water settle in your stomach first."

My head was spinning, but I didn't think it was due to my dehydration anymore.

"I don't need food right now," I told him. "I'm still trying to figure out why you're here. In Lania. None of this makes sense."

I was deliriously happy to hear his voice, but I still wasn't sure if any of this was real.

"I'm here to get you out of here," he said calmly as he propped his back against the metal support beam. "Emma, I've known Brock, Nate, Gage, and Seth for a long time, and I've known Wyatt Durand even longer. The guys were worried when you didn't check in. When I found out that you were in Lania, I called Nick. He told me the whole story about how you were kidnapped. That's why I'm here."

I took a moment to digest that information.

Okay, so he knew a lot of the same people I did, which explained a few things. "But how is you giving yourself up willingly going to get us out of here?"

I also wondered why he was doing this for a woman he hadn't seen in way over a decade.

"I know this hellhole isn't bugged," Colin answered. "This isn't a very sophisticated operation. So we can talk freely. I have a tracking device. Wyatt is in San Diego tracking our location. By nightfall tomorrow, Brock and Nate will be here to get us out of here. Wyatt, Brock, Nate, Gage, and Seth all work with me, Emma. We're all part of a private rescue organization that I founded years ago that we call Last Hope. We've done too many hostage rescues to count over the years."

I shook my head in disbelief. "Wyatt is a billionaire. He owns a parent company with luxury products."

"He does," he confirmed patiently. "But he and four other billionaires also work with me on Last Hope. We're headquartered in San Diego. Wyatt and the guys in Michigan were all on the same Delta Force team."

I knew that, but they'd all been out of Delta for years.

I had no idea that they were still running some kind of covert rescue operations.

Suddenly, all of my friends' mysterious disappearances over the years were starting to make sense.

"Is that why they disappeared and reappear like ghosts sometimes?" I questioned softly.

"Yeah," Colin admitted. "Keeping that secret is important. Lives depend on keeping that information quiet. Last Hope will only survive as long as nobody knows we exist, and keeping Last Hope running saves a lot of people that can't be helped by the US Government."

"The government doesn't know that these operations exist?" I asked, trying desperately to put all of the information together.

"Officially, they don't," he said evasively.

"Meaning they do know but they won't officially acknowledge it?" I questioned.

"Something like that," he answered. "But your friends aren't military anymore, and we aren't government. We don't step on their toes, and they ignore our existence for the most part."

"I have so many questions," I said honestly. "But I think I need to take in all of this crazy information first."

"It's a lot," he agreed. "Just know that by tomorrow night we'll be headed back to the US. We'll talk about the details later. I hate that this happened to you, Emma, and I really hate those bruises on your face. Why did those bastards have to rough you up?"

"I wouldn't answer their questions. They think I'm some secret girlfriend of Nick's, and I wouldn't confirm or deny. I thought it was better to let them think what they wanted. If I admitted I was nothing more than a friend to Nick, I was afraid they'd kill me because I wasn't as valuable to them. They weren't happy with my silence. I'm fine, Colin. Nothing is broken. They just bruised me up a little."

"Did they touch you in any other way?" he asked tersely.

"If you're asking if they raped me, they didn't. I've barely seen them since they tossed me in here. They were drugging me, but that stopped. God, I can't believe you're here and I'm actually going to live through this. I also can't believe that you just gave yourself up to locate me. That's completely insane."

I swiped a lone tear from my cheek. Now that the shock was wearing off, I was flooded with intense relief.

Yeah, I was upset that he'd just put his own life in danger to locate me, but I wasn't going to lie to myself and say that I wasn't glad that he was with me right now.

The water he'd brought had probably saved my life.

For some reason, I felt safe now that Colin was here, even if he did seem a little distant.

Honestly, what did I expect? We were strangers to each other now.

Colin had always been gruff and stoic, but I sensed that he'd changed a little.

There was more of an edginess to him that hadn't existed when I'd known him years ago.

"Are you crying?" he asked.

"Just a little," I confessed. "I guess I'm relieved that I'm not going to die here. I'm not sure how much longer I could have held out without water. Thank you for coming for me."

"It's what we do," he said casually. "We've been doing it for a long time."

"You've been doing it forever," I corrected. "I know we agreed not to share personal information in Virginia Beach, but I'm sure you were military, and I suspect you were probably special forces."

"Why did you think that?" he questioned.

I shrugged. "You're the most hypervigilant guy I've ever met. And you were intense. It was just a guess. Was I right?"

"Are we revealing our secrets now?" Colin asked cautiously.

"Why not?" I asked. "I already know one of your biggest secrets now about Last Hope. I promise I'll never tell anyone. I understand why it needs to stay a secret."

"I was a SEAL commander. I was stationed in Virginia Beach," he said grudgingly. "And I wasn't especially vigilant when I plowed you over on the sidewalk. I was fresh off a mission, and I was still reviewing everything we did in my head."

"Yeah, you seemed pretty uptight that first day," I agreed. "I'm not sure I would have accepted your invitation to have a drink if you hadn't seemed so…troubled and serious."

"Did you feel sorry for me?" he asked, sounding disgruntled.

Maybe it was a little weird for us to be talking about the past, but it was certainly better than worrying about dying here in Lania before we could be rescued.

INEVITABLE

Talking to Colin and discussing things we'd never talked about in Virginia Beach was a good distraction for me.

"No," I said truthfully. "But my instincts told me that I could trust you. Those instincts were right. So when did you retire from the military?"

I wasn't the type of woman who accepted invitations from strangers, but something about Colin had drawn me to him.

I realized almost immediately that we had some incredible chemistry that I'd never experienced before.

Seconds ticked by, and Colin didn't answer my question.

It was a simple question, but something told me that the answer must be…complicated.

CHAPTER 6

Marshall

The question should have been easy to answer, but I really didn't want to talk about my injury right now.

Hell, I never wanted to talk about it, but it wasn't like Emma wasn't going to notice once we stepped out of this shithole.

Since I didn't want to explain my injury when we were hightailing it for safety, it was better to tell her now.

"I had to retire early," I told her in a clipped voice. "Not long after you and I met in Virginia Beach. I was injured on my next mission. They managed to save my leg, but I couldn't continue with my duties as a SEAL commander after I recovered. I have a pretty bad limp, and my leg is a mess."

"Oh, God, Colin," she said, sounding horrified. "Tell me honestly, how bad was it?"

Fuck! I lied my ass off every single day when I was doing my job and gathering information, but I'd never been able to lie to Emma. "Pretty bad. I almost bled to death before I got to a hospital. I really don't remember that much after the injury. I was unconscious until I woke up from my first surgery. That was the first of several surgeries. I was in the hospital and then rehab for a long time."

Emma reached out and put her hand on my forearm to comfort me. "That must have been difficult emotionally and physically. I'm so sorry, Colin."

It had been forever since this woman had touched me, but I still felt that same spark of awareness that I really didn't want to feel fourteen years later.

It had always been that way with Emma, but it wasn't fucking possible that I still felt that awareness of her all these years later.

It had to be some kind of memory response.

"It's not your fault," I said stoically. "You weren't the one who tried to kill me."

"I'm sorry you had to go through that pain. I wish I could have been there for you."

"No, you don't," I said morosely. "I was a prick, Emma. I hated my life, and I was a miserable person to be around. My job as a SEAL commander meant everything to me. The only thing that got me through that time was pure stubbornness. I wanted to get as healthy as possible, even if I couldn't be a SEAL commander anymore. That injury changed me. I'm not the same man you knew fourteen years ago."

"Yes, you are," she said stubbornly. "You're still a guy who's willing to give yourself up for someone else. You're still putting other people before yourself. Don't tell me you're not the same man. You've been dedicating yourself to helping other people with Last Hope. Difficult times might change us, but you're still the same guy. You found another purpose in life. Maybe you couldn't be a SEAL commander, but you found a way to do something else that's meaningful to you."

I let out an exasperated breath as I reached for her food. "You always did try to find something positive in everything. Eat. You're going to need some energy for tomorrow night."

She took the pouch and the spoon I put into her hands.

I'd eaten MREs for years out in the field, and most of them tasted like crap, but I knew it was the most nutritious thing I could give her.

Luckily, the light was so dim that she couldn't see what that food looked like.

"It's good," she said after she'd tried it. "It's something Italian."

I let out a sharp bark of laughter. "You're only saying that because you've gone three days without food."

"You're probably right," she admitted. "Any food would taste good right now. How long is the hike out of here? I was so drugged that I don't really remember how far it was to get here."

I really fucking hated to think about the way Emma had been treated by her captors.

Yeah, I'd been relieved that she wasn't raped, but those bruises on her face had made me want to kill the bastards that had left those marks on her face.

They'd also given her enough drugs to make her forget her trip to this shithole.

She could have died from an overdose.

"We'll have to hike to get to a clearing where Nick can pick us up in his helicopter. The woods surrounding us are pretty dense. He'll fly us to the airport to board the private jets that will get us home."

"Private jets?" she asked in a surprised voice. "Exactly how big and technical is Last Hope?"

"Later," I said. "Right now we need to focus on getting you out of here."

There would be plenty of time on the flight home to answer those questions.

Once I knew that Emma was safe.

"What are Brock and Nate going to do about the kidnappers?"

"It's a stealth rescue," I explained. "They'll come in after the kidnappers are asleep and get us out of here without them ever knowing. The kidnappers aren't camping that close to this building, and your friends are masters at getting in and out without anyone knowing. They'll both be armed, but they won't use those weapons unless absolutely necessary. Nick will deal with those assholes after you're safely out of here."

"He'll still be in danger," she told me. "I think these guys are just hired thugs. His enemies will still be out there."

"Nick is aware of that," I said grimly. "He's hoping he can get the information he needs from the kidnappers."

Sadly, we really needed to leave that group of idiots alive so Nick could get to his actual enemies.

"You're injured. How are you going to hike out of here?" she queried softly.

"I might be old, and I have a limp," I said defensively. "But I'll hike out of here the same way I hiked in. I'm fit, even if I do have a limp."

"I'm sorry," she said, sounding contrite. "I was just worried. And I know you're not old. Do we want to share our ages now?"

"I'm fifty-three. I already know that you're forty-five," I explained. "Brock told me. You've always looked a lot younger than you are. I knew you were at least of drinking age when we met because you showed your ID at the bar where we had a drink, but you looked pretty young. You still do. I've seen some recent pictures. I felt old after seeing your picture. You haven't changed much."

"I've changed," she argued. "I'm not the same woman you knew years ago, either. I gained weight, and I feel old every time I look in the mirror. My life is very different than it was fourteen years ago. I lived in Chicago when we met. I was born and raised in Cherry Cove, so that's where I eventually decided to settle."

"You never found the man of your dreams?" I asked, already knowing it was something I didn't really need to know.

"No," she answered solemnly. "I was newly divorced when we met in Virginia Beach. My ex decided he wanted a younger woman after seven years of being married to me. Marriage hasn't exactly been high on my list of priorities. The first one wasn't a good experience for me."

"He was an idiot," I told her roughly.

Christ! What kind of simpleton would dump Emma for someone else? If I'd been a normal guy who wanted to get married, she would have been my dream woman.

"He was," she said with humor in her voice. "I was pretty young and naïve when we got married. I was an emotional mess by the time I divorced. Meeting you was the best thing that could have happened to me. You made me feel like a desirable woman again. I needed to feel that way at that point in my life, Colin."

"You were always a desirable woman," I said hoarsely. "You were everything any guy could ask for, Emma. Beautiful. Intelligent. Kind. Compassionate. That asshole must have done a number on you if you didn't know that."

"He did," she agreed. Emma was silent for a moment before she added, "You should have woken me up before you left. We never really got to say goodbye, and I never had a chance to thank you for the necklace."

Hell, I wasn't about to explain that I was afraid I'd change my mind about not exchanging information if I had woken her up that morning. "It was easier that way," I replied. "I'm not exactly good with emotional goodbyes, and we made a deal."

I saw her hand move to her neck before I asked, "You still have that necklace?"

"I've worn it almost every day since you gave it to me," she admitted. "I loved it. I still do. It was a pretty expensive gift for a fling. Gifts weren't exactly part of our deal, either."

Fuck! I suddenly hated the way she referred to herself as just a fling. "You were never just a woman I fucked for five days, Emma," I said as I ran my hand through my hair in frustration. "Our time together in Virginia Beach meant more to me than just that. Maybe I didn't know a lot about you or even your last name, but you meant something to me. I was married to the Navy at the time, but for just a short time, I forgot about my job and just spent as much time as I could with you. That had never happened to me before."

"It wasn't just a fling for me, either," she confessed. "That time meant something to me, too. I wasn't a woman who had ever even thought about having a fling or a one-night stand before we met. You probably already know my last name now. What's yours?"

"I know your last name," I confirmed. "My last name is Marshall. Everyone knows me as Marshall. I very rarely use my first name."

"Colin Marshall," she said like she was testing my full name out loud. "Wyatt mentioned knowing a guy named Marshall. That was you?"

"Yeah. I'm known by everyone as just Marshall at Last Hope."

"It's weird, right?" she asked in a contemplative voice. "All this time, we knew a lot of the same people, but we never ran into each other again."

I shrugged. "Maybe not so weird. I live in San Diego. You live in Michigan. I almost never leave San Diego because I like to be near Last Hope headquarters in case something comes up. I've never been to Cherry Cove. I've only seen our Michigan team in person on their infrequent visits to San Diego."

"Yet I've heard Wyatt describe you as the most intelligent person he's ever met, and I never knew he was referring to you," she replied. "That's weird for me."

It was odd for me to hear that Wyatt had said that to her.

I guess I'd never really wondered what my guys said about me when I wasn't around.

"I've been to San Diego," she mentioned. "My mother retired there a few years ago. She has friends there, and the winters in Cherry Cove were getting to her. I get there as often as I can."

"It's a big city," I reminded her. "It's not unusual that we've never run into each other. I spend most of my time at headquarters or at home. I'm not exactly a social kind of guy."

"What about dating?" she asked in a curious voice. "You haven't had a serious relationship?"

"Negative," I told her. "I'm about as eager to marry as you are. Never married. I never wanted to get married. I've watched every single one of my billionaire partners in San Diego lose their shit over a woman before they married their spouses. I've never had the desire to be in their positions."

Emma sighed. "I think Brock, Nate, Gage, and Seth feel the same way. But I think they're all lonely. I wish they'd find women who could make them happy."

"Why does everyone assume that a bachelor is lonely?" I questioned drily. "Maybe we just prefer our own company."

"I'm not saying all bachelors are lonely," she corrected. "But I know my friends. I've known them all for years, and I do think that they're lonely."

"Most of their spare time is probably consumed by Last Hope," I observed. "They're my most active team."

"They do disappear a lot," Emma observed. "I worry about them every time it happens."

"They trust you," I said. "But it's always been policy not to share information about Last Hope with anyone except significant others or kidnapping victims. It wasn't their fault. If it helps, those guys save a lot of lives when they disappear."

"It helps," she said earnestly. "I'm almost glad I didn't know that they were disappearing into dangerous situations."

I wanted to tell her that what those men did wasn't that dangerous to make her feel better, but that would have been a lie.

Every operative knew what they were getting themselves into when they went on a mission for Last Hope.

They knew the dangers, and they took them on willingly.

We took every precaution we could, but I couldn't say that it wasn't dangerous.

I handed Emma another packet from the MRE and decided to just remain silent.

Just like I always did.

I was a man of few words.

I'd discussed more personal things today than I had in years, and it was probably better to keep my mouth shut.

CHAPTER 7

Emma

"Sleep, Emma," Colin insisted later in the day. "You're going to need to be rested for tomorrow."

We'd spent the rest of the day catching up on trivial things, but at some point, I knew Colin and I had to have a serious talk.

Now wasn't the time, but I'd made him promise that he wouldn't just disappear before we had a chance to have a discussion like he'd done the last time.

He'd agreed before we'd stopped talking to try to get some sleep.

Colin didn't seem to have any aversion to spreading out on the ground next to me.

I was still propped against the support beam.

"I've had problems sleeping since I've been here. That concrete floor is disgusting, and I don't sleep well sitting up," I shared.

"I hate to admit that I slept in worse places when I was an active SEAL," Colin replied. "I was trained to sleep in any environment. I spread the blanket out next to me so you don't have to rest on the dirty floor. Sleep."

Colin had offered me a blanket earlier, but it wasn't exactly cold in this place, so I'd told him I didn't need it.

I shuddered. "It's not just the filth that bothers me," I admitted. "I saw a rat in here, Colin. It ran right over my leg. I hate rodents. I know that probably sounds ridiculous to you considering our situation, but I don't want them chewing on my face when I'm sleeping. The thought of it just creeps me out."

"You've been kidnapped, starved, and deprived of food and water. You say that you're fine after taking a few beatings, but you're worried about the rodents?" he asked with something that sounded suspiciously like amusement.

"I know it sounds stupid," I said, disgusted. "But I can't help it. Rats freak me out."

"It's not stupid," Colin said calmly as he wrapped an arm around me and pulled me down beside him. "But you have to sleep, Emma. Use me. I'll keep the rats away."

He settled my head on his broad chest, and I let out a quiet sigh.

The blanket felt like heaven under my body, and I felt even safer when he wrapped a powerful arm around me.

Colin was dressed just like I was in a T-shirt and jeans. We didn't have a lot of skin-to-skin contact, but feeling his warm, muscular body beside me was still comforting.

It was also a little disconcerting.

Like it or not, my body still reacted the same way it had to Colin years ago.

One touch.

One whiff of his masculine scent, and I wanted to get this man naked.

I was exhausted, but my body instantly responded in a carnal way.

It was ridiculous, but all of the memories of all the times we'd had the best sex of my life flooded into my head.

My response to him *couldn't* be real.

I was a different person than I'd been all those years ago.

It had been fourteen years.

It was probably just a muscle memory reaction.

We hadn't been together in fourteen years, and I couldn't say that I'd had a carnal instinct toward anyone since I'd been with Colin in Virginia Beach.

Being like this with Colin felt oddly familiar, even though we hadn't laid this close together for many years.

His body felt just as rock solid as it had years ago.

I rested my hand on his abdomen, which confirmed that he was still as ripped as he'd been in Virginia Beach.

The man might be in his fifties now, but he was still incredibly fit.

"I wish I was still in the shape I was in when we were together," I blurted out as I snuggled against him. "I've put on weight."

"You're still just as attractive," Colin said earnestly. "Why are you worried about being curvier? It suits you."

"I was post-divorce thin back when we met. Now I struggle with my weight. The older I get the harder it is to maintain a healthy weight. I walk and I swim in the summer, but it's a struggle. How do you keep in shape?"

"I have pool at home," he shared. "It's heated so I can swim in all seasons in San Diego. I also have a gym at home, which makes keeping in shape easier. I hike when I can get out. I never really got out of the habit of exercising after being a SEAL for so many years."

"I've always been a little plump," I shared with Colin. "The only time I was really thin was right after my divorce. I was diagnosed with PCOS after I was married. It's really hard for me to lose weight."

"Polycystic ovary syndrome?" he asked. "Why didn't you mention that when we were together in Virginia Beach?"

It didn't really surprise me that Colin knew exactly what PCOS was and what that abbreviation stood for.

The guy had a genius IQ and a photographic memory.

If he read something about a subject just once, he remembered it forever.

"It wasn't really that important," I responded. "It wasn't like I was sick from it. It was just a condition I had."

"Are you okay now?" he asked with concern in his voice.

My heart warmed as he asked that question.

Just like my heart had warmed when he'd pulled out a bag of peppermints for me earlier that he'd brought from home to cheer me up.

We hadn't seen each other in years, but he obviously still cared about my personal well-being.

It was little things that Colin did that made me not completely buy into his tough guy attitude.

He might act unemotional, but he definitely had a heart. He might not wear it on his sleeve, but it was there.

"I'm fine. I've been on birth control for years to control the symptoms, but that definitely doesn't help me lose weight."

"You exercise," he pointed out. "You're healthy, and you look beautiful, Emma. You don't need to be thin like you were in Virginia Beach."

Ha! That was easy for him to say. He was still just as fit as he was when he was fourteen years younger.

I, on the other hand, was plump compared to the time when we were sleeping together in Virginia Beach.

"I don't think I'll ever be that thin again. I was such a mess that I barely ate," I said with a sigh. "I like food too much to give it up. I just try to eat healthy most of the time."

"Hey, at least you don't have a limp and a mangled leg," he said in a self-deprecating tone.

"Don't say that," I said, unamused. "You got that injury serving our country."

I still hated the fact that I hadn't been there for him when it happened.

It had happened so close to the time that we'd been together in Virginia Beach.

Grump or not, he'd needed someone, and no one had really been there for him except members of his SEAL team.

While we were catching up earlier, Colin had mentioned that he'd been a foster child, so he hadn't even had family beside him throughout that horrible ordeal.

"Does that make my limp more noble?" he asked soberly.

"Stop that," I insisted. "I hate it when you talk about that injury like it was nothing. It turned your life upside down and it caused you a lot of pain."

"It happened years ago, Emma," he said soothingly. "It just feels new to you because you just found out about it. I've learned to live with it and the limitations it puts on my body."

"You're right," I admitted. "I'm sorry. I just hate the pain you must have gone through. Do you want to talk about what happened?"

"It's all classified," he said stoically. "But I can say it was a screwed-up mission from the start. Anything that could go wrong did go wrong. I was monitoring the operations from nearby when I got word the place was rigged with IEDs. My guys were running into a trap. Our communications system died, so there was no other way to warn them except for me hauling ass to their location before they all got blown up. I had no choice but to run through the area that was rigged to head them off. Luckily, no one hit one of those landmines except me. I waved my guys back. I thought I was home free myself, but my luck ran out on those last few steps out of that trap. Actually, I was lucky. They told me later that my foot hit just the right way to keep me from losing my life and not just the normal use of my leg. Most of my body escaped injury except for my leg. That's not what usually happens when a bomb is pressure sensitive."

Dear God! The man had actually run through landmines to save his team.

"You knew you could die doing what you did," I said shakily.

"I did," he confirmed. "But it was better to lose one guy than a whole damn team. I was their commander. I sent them into that shitshow. It was my job to get them out alive if I could."

I understood his sense of responsibility and moral obligation, but…

"That was completely insane," I told him. "You weren't afraid you were going to die?"

"I didn't have time to think much about that," he explained. "The whole scene was chaotic. I just did what I had to do."

What kind of bravery did it take to just run into a dangerous situation like that without thinking about it?

But I knew it didn't simply take incredible bravery to do what Colin did.

It took…heart.

He'd cared about the guys under his command, and he'd put the lives of those men before his own.

"You're an amazing man, Colin Marshall," I said honestly.

"I was just doing my job, Emma. I knew what I signed up for when I became a SEAL."

It was risky as hell, but he'd still signed up knowing how dangerous it could be for him.

My admiration for Colin had reached new heights.

Yeah, I'd suspected he was military, but I'd never known his life was probably in danger on a daily basis.

I realized just how much I hadn't known about him back in Virginia Beach.

We'd known each other's bodies, but there were so many things we *hadn't* shared.

"Sleep, Emma," Colin said as he ran a comforting hand over my hair. "We can talk more once I get you to safety. That's my main concern right now. The hike out of here isn't going to be easy, and you've been through a lot over the last three days."

I let out an exasperated breath.

Probably no one on Earth had been through more than Colin, yet he was still worried about *my* safety.

His concern for hostages had probably been ingrained in him throughout his time as a SEAL.

Strangely, I hadn't had a moment of fear since the moment I'd heard his voice.

Yeah, I was apprehensive about escaping, but being with Colin had pushed most of the dark thoughts right out of my head.

It was probably his calmness and his confidence.

He was treating this situation like something he'd done many times, which he probably had.

"I'll be fine," I told him. "I've done long hikes in the woods before. I've lived in Michigan most of my life."

"You didn't do those hikes half-starved and sleep deprived," he pointed out. "You're physically depleted, Emma."

I let out a yawn before I said, "Okay, I'm sleeping."

Surprisingly, comfortable with being held tightly by Colin, I was doing just that a few moments later.

CHAPTER 8

Marshall

"How did it go?" Emma asked anxiously after the kidnapper had reattached me to the support beam and left our prison the next morning.

I'd spent the last two hours in the kidnappers' camp going through the motions of negotiating Nick's release.

I'd thrown out some ridiculous and outrageous terms deliberately because I knew they weren't going to immediately agree.

They were going to come back with what their bosses would agree to in the morning.

That worked for me.

We would be long gone, and those assholes would be in custody.

"It was fine. I threw out a whole lot of bullshit."

I was used to that. I did it nearly every day as a contractor and intel gatherer for the US government.

"They didn't hurt you?" she asked nervously as she ran her hands over my face to make sure I was okay.

Fuck! I was developing a love/hate relationship with her being this close to me.

I hadn't slept worth a damn.

Emma had drifted off to sleep.

Me?

I'd held her while my dick reminded me that it was still fully functional, even if I was a lot older than I had been when Emma and I had first met.

I shouldn't, but I still wanted Emma just as much as I had back then.

She still smelled the same.

She still felt like the only woman who could make me completely lose my head.

Personally, I happened to like her curvier body, and so did my cock.

She'd gotten a little restless in her sleep, and I'd instinctively put a hand on her ass to calm her just like I'd done in Virginia Beach.

Okay, I'd eventually moved my hand away, but my dick had gotten even harder than it had been before I'd made that mistake.

My attraction to Emma wasn't *simply* muscle memory.

Hell, I still wanted her even though I knew it was wrong.

The more I got to know her personally, the stronger that attraction was growing.

Everyone in my life treated me with a healthy amount of respect most of the time.

Emma had never feared me.

She wasn't wary of me.

She wasn't afraid to give me hell when she thought I deserved it.

That had intrigued me back then, and it fascinated me now.

I was a big, stoic, gruff, and humorless kind of guy who never talked about anything emotional.

None of those traits had ever seemed to bother her.

She hadn't blinked an eye when I'd told her that I had a genius IQ and a photographic memory in Virginia Beach.

She'd simply…accepted me exactly the way I was.

She had never seen any of those things as odd or off-putting.

That's probably why I'd become so crazy about her in Virginia Beach.

She'd gotten closer to me than any woman ever had in my entire life.

I took her hand from my face and held it against my chest. "I'm fine. I fed them a bunch of bullshit, and it stalled things until tomorrow. By then, we'll be gone."

"Thank God," she said in a relieved voice.

"You were worried about me?" I asked.

That slayed me because Emma was the actual kidnapping victim. I was trained to deal with kidnappers.

She smacked me on the shoulder with her free hand. "Of course I was worried about you. We have no idea what these guys are capable of doing."

The last thing I wanted was to worry her because she'd already been through enough in the last several days. "Everything's fine, Emma. I'm fine. You sound stressed."

I pulled her down to sit with me on the blanket.

Without thinking, I wrapped my arm around her, and she put her head on my shoulder.

"Maybe I'm a little nervous about tonight," she confided.

"Don't be," I insisted. "Brock and Nate have never failed at a rescue mission, and you know Nick. He's reliable. He's helped me out before. The guy is eager to get you out of here, too. It's perfectly normal to be nervous, but don't let those fears get into your head."

"It's hard not to," she murmured against my shoulder. "What if I make noise and the kidnappers wake up? What if something goes wrong? What if I can't keep up with you guys?"

"Do you honestly think we're going to leave you behind?" I asked wryly. "You're the reason we're doing this. We're going to guide you every step of the way. We'll make sure you don't make a mistake, and we'll move at your pace. If something goes wrong, we always have plan B and plan C. Things do go wrong sometimes, but we know how to adapt. We'll take care of you, Emma. I'll make damn sure you get home safely to Cherry Cove."

"I trust all of you, but maybe I don't trust myself. I'm out of my depth here. It's my first kidnapping."

"It's also going to be your last," I grunted. "I'm getting too old to be out in the field. After years of doing this, I much prefer my comfortable bed and running operations from headquarters."

"Then why didn't you send one of those younger guys?" she asked.

"Because the kidnapping victim was you," I admitted freely. "I couldn't sit on the sidelines for this one. I told you that you weren't just a fling to me, Emma. Maybe we were only together for a short time, but those five days made a real impression on me."

"Me, too," she answered. "I regretted the deal we made after you were gone. I wish we would have stayed in touch. I was going to talk to you about it the morning you left. Maybe neither of us was in a position for something more, but I'd like to think we became friends."

"It was better the way it worked out," I replied. "I was never around for long, Emma, and I would have been a shitty friend. My whole life revolved around the Navy. I thought I was doing the right thing at the time, but for what it's worth, I had second thoughts about the deal, too. I swung by the beach house later that morning, but you were already gone."

"You came back looking for me?" she asked in a surprised voice.

"Yeah," I answered. "I was only back at base for a few hours before it hit me that I wanted to stay in touch, too. I didn't know where you lived but at least I could hear your voice on the phone once in a while."

I wasn't quite sure about the whole friendship thing. I doubted that I could watch Emma date other guys and make a life for herself with someone else, but I hadn't really thought that far into the future at the time.

It had just suddenly hit me that I was an idiot for walking away from the most incredible woman I'd ever met.

"I wish we would have met up before I left," she said regretfully. "I missed you after I left Virginia Beach."

"I missed you, too."

I was right the morning I'd left that beach house.

Thoughts of Emma *had* haunted me for a very long time.

I'd had my share of regrets about the way things had ended between us.

I'd often wondered exactly what would have happened if we had stayed in touch.

Probably nothing.

I'd changed after my injury, and I'd spent a long time recovering.

I'd pushed everyone away so I could wallow in my misery alone.

No doubt I would have pushed Emma away, too.

Over the years, I'd decided that the way things had ended between Emma and me had been for the best.

"We're going to keep in touch this time," Emma said in a stubborn voice.

"We will," I assured her. "I plan on being your assigned advisor after this is over. Last Hope never just cuts our victims loose after a kidnapping. Your confinement was short, but issues could pop up well after this is over. Even the bravest of captives suffer some PTSD. We have people who can help with that if you need it. I'm going to be there for you, Emma."

"I'm going to be there for you, too," she insisted. "I don't just want to keep in touch with some kind of advisor. I want to be your friend, Colin."

This time, I did smile.

A little.

As much as a guy like me was capable of smiling.

Emma was probably the most obstinate woman I'd ever known. When she got something into her head, she didn't let go.

Would it really hurt to go along with her plan?

Nope.

Truth was, I wanted to keep her in my life, too.

Screw my attraction to her.

I'd have to live with it because there was no way that Emma was going to feel that kind of attraction toward me.

I'd have to get the fuck over it if I wanted to keep her in my life.

"Agreed," I said.

"Can you stay with me for a little while once we get back to Cherry Cove?" she asked hesitantly.

The vulnerability in her voice got to me.

My immediate reaction would usually be to get back to San Diego and my headquarters as soon as possible.

That was my life.

I could do my contracting job anywhere as long as I had my computer.

Last Hope was another story.

I needed to be in our high-tech operations center.

It's not like Wyatt can't handle everything there if I'm gone for a while.

If Emma needed me, I could stay in Michigan.

I had committed to being her advisor.

"As long as you need me there," I promised, surprising myself because I really meant those words.

Emma came first at the moment.

For the first time in my life Last Hope and my contract work weren't my only priority.

Nothing would tear me away from Emma until I knew she was going to be okay on her own in Cherry Cove.

CHAPTER 9

Emma

I jumped a little at the sound of a bird outside the tiny window in our prison.

I'd been doing that since it had gotten dark.

Every little noise made me uptight.

Colin and I were laying together on the blanket, but I certainly wasn't sleeping.

I was nervous, even though I was trying hard not to be.

"Relax, Emma," Colin said soothingly next to my ear. "They'll be here as soon as the kidnappers are asleep."

I swallowed hard. My heart had been like a lump in my throat for the last hour.

I was afraid for my friends.

I was worried about Colin.

And I really needed to get home safe.

"I think I just want this to be over," I replied as I tried to force myself to relax.

Giving in to fear wasn't going to help our situation right now.

"Are you getting tired of eating those horrible MREs?" he asked jokingly, trying to make me relax.

I took a deep breath and let it out. "I'm more tired of using a bucket for a toilet," I said, trying to keep things light, too. "And I'll never take a hot shower for granted ever again."

I knew I was smelling pretty rank right now. I was dirty. I was sweaty during the day when it was hot in this filthy prison.

But Colin held me tightly anyway like he didn't notice any of those things.

"You'll get that shower," he promised. "Do you remember everything I told you?"

Remember?

Yeah, I recalled everything and those details had been running through my mind all evening.

Brock and Nate would come in and out without speaking.

Not a word would be said until we were out of hearing range of the kidnappers.

My first instinct would be to throw myself into the arms of my friends, but that reunion was going to have to wait until we were safely out of here.

You can do this, Emma. You can keep a cool head until everyone is safe.

Honestly, sometimes this whole thing felt surreal to me.

It was still hard for me to believe that two of my best friends were part of a very covert operation that rescued hostages.

I'd never even imagined that the two men who had been like brothers to me had this side of their life that I didn't know about.

To me, Brock was a friendly, best-selling novelist.

Nate was a creative, surreal landscape artist.

Gage owned the most popular beachfront restaurant in town.

And Seth...

Seth was different. He wasn't the friendly, outgoing guy his friends were because he was self-conscious about the scars he'd gotten on a mission gone wrong while he was in Delta.

He was quiet and a little more reclusive than the rest of the guys, but he had an amazing heart that not many people could see.

Still, it was hard for me to come to terms with the fact that they'd all been part of this secret life.

I wasn't upset that none of them had told me about Last Hope. I understood their need for secrecy.

But it still seemed…unreal.

Gage was a Michigander, born and raised in Cherry Cove. He'd come back home after he left Delta, and his friends had followed soon after to settle down with Gage in Michigan.

The guys were like brothers, so it wasn't surprising that they didn't want to end that bond simply because they were out of the military.

I heard a bird call softly again, and I forced myself not to react.

"They're coming in," Colin said in a quiet, harsh voice.

"How do you know that?" I whispered.

"That wasn't a bird. That's Nate," he answered as he stood and pulled me gently to my feet.

My heart started to pound so hard that I was afraid the kidnappers could hear that rapid beat.

Colin put the pack he'd brought on his back and took my hand. "Everything will be fine, Emma. Don't let go of my hand."

I nodded and swallowed hard even though I knew that Colin probably couldn't see that nod.

The guys would all be using night vision glasses, so I was going to have to keep close to Colin so he could lead me out of here.

Not that I planned on leaving his side anyway.

Right now, he was my lifeline, and I trusted him completely.

I heard the very faint sound at the door which was probably the guys picking the lock.

The moments seemed to stretch on forever until that door, which usually opened with a ton of noise, was almost silently pushed open enough for two men to enter the room.

Once the door was open, there was enough light from the moon and stars to see that both of them were dressed completely in black.

My heart squeezed, but I was silent as Brock and Nate approached us so stealthily that they didn't make a sound.

They made short work of our cuffs with some kind of tool that they must have brought with them.

Everything happened so fast.

One moment we were still shackled in our prison.

The next moment we were all outside and free.

I could see Brock making some hand signals after he'd handed Colin his night vision glasses, but nobody made a sound.

My hands were shaking as Colin affixed both of them to the waistband of his jeans so I could follow right behind him and not run into anything I couldn't see.

Brock and Nate took the lead, and we followed behind.

The moon wasn't full, but I had enough light to be able to see Colin's large form in front of me, and that was all I really needed to see.

Colin's gait was uneven because of his previous injury, but he was strong and steady as we made our way through the woods.

I willed myself to think only about my next step and getting to our destination.

We traveled that way for what seemed like a long time before Colin abruptly stopped.

Before I knew what was happening, I was pulled into Brock's arms and he hugged me so tightly I could barely breathe.

"Fuck, Emma!" he said quietly next to my ear. "You had us all pretty worried. Gage and Seth are on their way back home, but they're pretty frantic right now, too. You okay?"

"I'm okay," I assured him as my eyes filled with tears.

I was so damn happy to hear Brock's voice.

"My turn," Nate rumbled as he pulled me from Brock to give me a giant bear hug. "Are you sure you're okay?"

"A little scared, but physically I'm good," I told Nate. "Thank you both for coming for me and for helping Colin. The water he had with him probably saved my life."

"Who in the hell is Colin?" Brock questioned in a puzzled voice.

"It's me," Colin grumbled. "Can you two stop squeezing the life out of Emma? She needs to breathe, and her face is a little bruised. She took a few beatings at the hands of her kidnappers."

Nate reluctantly released me as he hissed, "That makes me wish we could have killed those bastards."

I patted him on the arm. "It doesn't hurt anymore. I really am alright, Nate."

"She knows you as Colin?" Brock asked. "Your name is Marshall."

"Colin Marshall," I informed my friends. "I've always known him as Colin."

"That's why she never asked about you when Wyatt talked about you," Brock muttered. "She didn't know your last name."

"I prefer to go by Marshall most of the time," Colin said sternly. "Emma was a rare exception."

I was glad he'd made that exception. I couldn't imagine calling a man I was sleeping with by his last name.

Maybe he didn't like it, but I happened to love his first name.

"How much farther is it to the clearing?" I asked.

"We still have a small trek ahead of us," Colin informed me. "Do you need to rest for a while?"

I was exhausted emotionally and physically. I'd been sedentary and unable to walk for days now, but I wanted to keep moving.

"I can walk," I told him. "Let's get the hell out of here."

"I second that," Nate said. "I don't think any of us are fond of this damn country. We've all been here too many times, and none of them were for anything pleasant."

As we all started the final trek, I thought about Nate's comment.

Lania had been a country engaged in a bitter civil war for a long time.

It made sense that the three men had all been here before.

They were all previous special forces.

Once the rebels had been forced out of Lania, Nick had tried to turn everything around.

I kind of wished that my friends could see the other side of the island nation.

It was beautiful and tropical.

I'd actually been enjoying my visit to Lania before the kidnapping had occurred.

I could see why tourists were flocking to the capital city and the surrounding beaches.

There were almost no signs of the previous civil war there, and it was the closest thing I'd seen to paradise.

"We're here," Brock said as we finally stopped in the middle of a clearing in the woods. "I already signaled Nick. I can hear the helicopter in the distance."

I took a deep breath and released it.

I could hear that helicopter, too, and it was the most beautiful sound I'd ever experienced.

I watched as the lights of the aircraft came into view, and as soon as it landed Colin boosted me into the helicopter.

I landed in the arms of a man I'd called my friend for several years now.

He put on the headset that I was already familiar with from my previous ride in the same helicopter.

"Emma," Nick said in a relieved voice as he hugged me. "Bloody hell! I was worried about you. I'm so sorry this happened to you. This was all my fault."

Prince Nick had a pronounced British accent because he'd spent most of his life in England. The king had sent his only son there to protect him from the dangers of the war in Lania.

"It wasn't your fault, Nick," I scolded him. "You had no way of knowing that someone was going to try to assassinate you."

I pulled back and looked at his handsome face.

Nick was younger than I was and incredibly handsome with his dark hair and beautiful brown eyes.

Unfortunately, that male beauty was marred by the stress he'd been through since the kidnapping.

He was dressed in a T-shirt and jeans, and he looked nothing like the crown prince that he actually was.

There was nothing pretentious about Nick.

Most of the time he preferred to act and dress like a normal guy.

"I brought you here," he said as the men boarded the helicopter. "I promised you it was safe."

"Lania is safe. This wasn't your fault, Nick. Stop blaming yourself. I'm fine."

"You're not fine," he answered in a disgruntled voice. "Did those assholes hit you? Your face is bruised."

I shook my head. "It doesn't hurt. It just looks bad. I'm good and I'll be even better if you get me out of this area. Where are your bodyguards?"

Nick finally grinned. "Back at the palace. I didn't give them a choice. I told them there was no room for them. They were somewhat satisfied that I'd have three previous special forces guys to protect me."

I smiled at him and moved to the back seat to make more space for Colin, Brock, and Nate.

Nick motioned to the pilot when the door closed, and I could tell we were getting ready to lift off.

Colin, Brock, and Nate donned their headsets, and Colin dropped into the seat beside me in the back.

The lights were on, and for the very first time, I got a very good look at his face.

As usual, when those steel gray eyes of his pierced me, I felt like he could see all the way to my soul.

Yes, he was a little older, but my heart skipped a beat and my breath caught as he looked at me with concern.

There was a little bit of gray in the stubble on his face and a little sprinkled in his brown hair.

Unfortunately, I found that incredibly sexy.

One thing hadn't changed.

He was still the handsomest man on the planet.

As the helicopter lifted off, relief like I'd never felt before flooded my entire body.

We were all going to live through this.

No one got hurt.

We were going home.

Tears filled my eyes, and to my mortification, I threw myself in Colin's arms and started to sob like a child.

CHAPTER 10

Marshall

I knew Emma was going through the aftereffects of the kidnapping. She hadn't whined about her fate. She hadn't really cried.

Emma had put on a brave face while the situation was happening, but all of those emotions had to go somewhere at some point in time.

I wrapped my arms around her and let her cry, and the permafrost that usually surrounded my heart melted just a little while she did.

Nick, Brock, and Nate turned around, their faces concerned, but I shook my head subtly.

Emma was vulnerable right now, and I didn't want anyone to console her except me.

They nodded and turned around.

"I'm sorry," Emma said as the sobs subsided. "I guess I got emotional now that I know that none of us are going to get hurt."

"Don't be sorry," I told her as I stroked my hand over her back. "The reaction is perfectly normal. You've kept all of your emotions bottled up for days. What you went through would be a nightmare experience for anyone. Those emotions eventually have to come out or they'll eat you alive."

She leaned back a little. "I don't see you crying."

I heard Brock and Nate snicker a little, but I ignored it. "I don't cry," I grumbled. "And I'm trained for this sort of thing. I was the rescuer. You were the victim."

"I don't think I like being a victim of any kind." She sniffled. "I'm used to taking care of myself. This whole situation was a lot. Nick was nearly assassinated, and you, Brock, and Nate had to put yourselves in danger just to rescue me."

"I'm alive, Emma," Nick said calmly through the headphones without turning his head to look at her. "Once I find out who my enemies are and eliminate the threat, I'll be safe. Bloody hell! I was more worried about your safety than mine. I had bodyguards who kept me safe. You were vulnerable and snatched because I wasn't vigilant enough about your safety."

"We weren't really in danger," Nate added. "We do this kind of thing a lot. We know what we're doing."

"You aren't invulnerable," she argued.

"We know that," Brock informed me. "But we take a lot of precautions. And it was probably Marshall who really saved your life. I didn't like the thought of him surrendering himself. I knew we could eventually get your location, but you didn't have that kind of time. I thought the assholes would at least keep you hydrated."

"They didn't even give you water?" Nick asked gruffly.

"Almost none," she admitted reluctantly.

"I'll make those assholes pay for nearly killing you, and for those bruises on your face. I guess I'm indebted once again to the operatives of Last Hope and to Marshall."

Emma shot me a questioning look.

"Long story about my billionaire partners' wives. They were both American geologists who almost died here after being kidnapped by some random rebels. But they lived, married their billionaires, and lived happily ever after. You don't need the details of that ordeal right now."

Emma just needed to relax and think about something more positive, like the fact that we were going home.

"You'll be getting that hot shower soon," I reminded her.

She pulled back from me a little. "Thank God. I probably stink."

I pulled her back against me. "You're fine."

The bruises on her face made me livid; her hair was a little matted, and she looked a little rough from her ordeal, but she was still beautiful.

Her gorgeous blue eyes were still just as mesmerizing as they'd always been.

"I just got word that my military has the kidnappers in custody," Nick mentioned.

"That was fast," Emma commented.

"They were in place and ready to sweep in as soon as all of you were safely gone," Nick commented. "If all goes well, I'll have my enemies contained soon."

"How is the king?" Emma asked softly.

"Still fighting off a very bad case of pneumonia, but the doctors are hopeful," Nick said solemnly.

The Lanian king might be demented, but it was a relief for me to hear that he might live. Nick loved his father, and he'd told me recently that he wasn't ready to be the king.

It was easier for him to be the unofficial ruler for now. He could keep a lower profile and work on all the changes that needed to be made in Lania.

In my opinion, he'd make a great leader, but Nick had spent a lot of time in England before he'd come back to Lania several years ago. He needed more experience dealing with the politics of the monarchy.

"Are you sure you don't want to rest up at the palace for a while?" Nick offered in a sincere voice. "I'd be honored to have you all as my guests."

"No offense intended," Brock said. "But I never want to stay in Lania longer than absolutely necessary."

Nick chuckled. "No offense taken, mate. I know none of you have a good history here, but you're welcome to be my guest any time you'd like. I'd like to show you the better side of Lania."

"Some other time maybe," Nate said unenthusiastically.

"I'd like to get Emma back home as soon as possible," I told Nick. "She needs to recover in a place where she feels safe."

"I loved what I saw of Lania, Nick," Emma said gently. "It's beautiful here. I'd like to come back someday after the political situation is stable. Please keep me posted with news about the kidnappers and updates on your dad."

"You have an open invitation," Nick said charmingly. "Having a gorgeous woman like you around the palace is always going to brighten up the place."

I gritted my teeth.

Nick was a charming guy. It was part of his persona as a prince. But I could do without him charming Emma.

"Are you and Emma taking Wyatt's jet back?" Brock questioned.

"Yeah," I confirmed. "You and Nate can fly back with Jax's jet."

Brock let out a snort of laughter. "That's not exactly a hardship. I think Jax's jet is even more elaborate than Wyatt's."

Emma shot me a puzzled look. "Exactly how many private jets do you have at your disposal?"

"Five," all of us said in unison.

"All five of my billionaire partners have their own jet," I explained.

"Last Hope sounds like a pretty complicated operation," Emma mused.

"Moreso than you can imagine," Brock said with a chuckle. "There's probably more high-tech equipment at headquarters than the government has at its disposal. Some of it was designed by Marshall. He's also one of our secret weapons because he's one of the best hackers and intel experts on the planet."

Emma tilted her head as she looked at me. "Is that true?"

"He's exaggerating," I grumbled.

"No, he's not," Nate chimed in. "It's the absolute truth. That's why he's the boss. That and the fact that he actually founded Last Hope. Don't get me wrong, we need Wyatt, Hudson, Jax, Cooper, and Chase, but Last Hope wouldn't exist without Marshall."

Emma lifted an eyebrow.

"Last Hope needs every member to function the way it does," I said sternly, trying to get the guys to keep their opinions to themselves.

"Is everything still quiet at headquarters?" I asked, trying to change the subject.

"Extremely quiet," Brock confirmed. "But we all know that can change in a hurry. Are you staying in Cherry Cove for at least a few days?"

"I'm staying," I confirmed. "I'm going to be Emma's advisor. I want to make sure she's recovered from this before I go. Wyatt's in charge until further notice. I'll contact him as soon as we get back to Michigan."

"You better call your mom, Emma. She was frantic," Brock said.

"My mother knows about this?" Emma squeaked, sounding alarmed.

"We didn't tell her," Nate promised. "She called us when you stopped answering your texts."

"I'll call as soon as we get home," she said hastily, sounding worried.

"I hated to do it, but I gave her a few bullshit excuses. We said that you were traveling to a more remote area of Lania to sightsee and probably wouldn't have cell coverage for a few days," Brock explained. "We didn't want to tell her the truth until we knew you were safely home."

"Thanks for covering for me," Emma replied in a relieved voice.

"You owe us," Nate said jokingly. "It's not easy lying to your mom. She adores us and we'd like to keep it that way."

"She'll still adore you all," Emma teased. "She thinks none of you can do any wrong."

It suddenly occurred to me that my Michigan team knew far more about Emma's life than I did.

They were even close to her mother.

Rationally, that made sense because Emma had mentioned that her mother had retired just a few years ago.

My team had been in Michigan for a long time, so they'd probably had a good relationship with Emma's mother before she'd moved to California.

They were probably well acquainted with *everyone* who was important in Emma's life.

I literally knew nothing about Emma's life except for the things I'd learned about her in Virginia Beach and during our two days together recently.

I'll learn more about her in Cherry Cove.

We'd been thrown together in a stressful situation.

There hadn't been a lot of time to learn about what her life was like and the woman she was now.

Getting to know her was going to be necessary if I was going to be her advisor.

"We're getting closer to the airport," Nick informed us. "It won't be long now."

"Please take care of yourself, Nick," Emma pleaded. "I'll be worried about you until all of this is resolved. Let your bodyguards stay close to you."

"Like I have a choice?" he answered drily. "I have no doubt they'll be waiting for me at the airport now that there will be enough room in the helicopter."

"They're dedicated to protecting you," Emma reminded him. "Just let them do their job. Please."

"How can I deny that request from a beautiful woman like you?" Nick said suavely.

"You can't," Emma said firmly. "And drop the charm, mister. I'm completely immune to that bullshit. We've known each other for a long time. Don't try to placate me. Promise me that you'll be as safe as possible. I almost watched you die from an assassination attempt."

"I promise," Nick said contritely and completely without the sophisticated charm.

"Good," Emma said in a satisfied voice.

It took everything I had not to really smile this time.

Emma was probably the gutsiest woman I'd ever known.

Friend or not, Nick *was* a crown prince, and Emma had just bitched him out for not taking his safety seriously.

She did that a lot. She'd do it to me, too, if she thought I needed a wakeup call.

No wonder I'd been crazy about her in Virginia Beach.

She was the sweetest woman in the world until someone really pissed her off.

But her claws came out when she was worried about someone.

Hell, I was probably screwed because I still thought her protectiveness with the people she cared about was the sexiest thing I'd ever seen.

CHAPTER 11

Emma

I felt like a new woman a few hours later as I sat on the massive bed in the master bedroom of Wyatt's private jet.

My best friend, Sara, had packed some things for me and sent them with Brock and Nate.

She'd included everything I could have wanted…clean clothing, my summer nightgown, my toothbrush, some of my favorite lotions, and my makeup bag.

As soon as we'd reached cruising altitude, I'd headed for the luxurious bathroom attached to the master bedroom.

I'd washed my shoulder-length hair more than once and scrubbed my entire body at least three times.

For the first time in days, I felt clean.

I'd probably never take that feeling for granted again.

Colin and I had eaten with Brock and Nate before we'd taken off on separate flights, so my belly was full.

I was thoroughly exhausted, but my mind was still racing with a million different thoughts.

However, every one of those thoughts left my head as Colin walked out of the bathroom after his shower.

He was wearing a pair of jeans but no shirt.

Dear God, how was it possible that he still had a droolworthy body in his fifties?

His six-pack abs were still pronounced, and his chiseled shoulders, chest, and arms were ridiculous.

My heart skipped a beat as he shot me a questioning look, probably because I was staring at him like an idiot.

I forced my gaze away from him, but it wasn't easy.

I'd always thought that Colin was the sexiest man on Earth, and that certainly hadn't changed.

Even after fourteen years, it was hard for me to look at him and not want him naked.

I ached to touch him, but I had to remind myself that all of that was in our past.

We were different people now.

"What exactly does a Last Hope advisor do?" I asked curiously, trying to get my mind off my lingering attraction to Colin.

I hadn't seen him in fourteen years, so it was probably normal that I associated Colin with incredible sex.

He *had* been the man who had taught me that I was more than capable of feeling desire and passion on a whole different level.

"It means I'll be in your life for a while," Colin answered as he reached into a duffle bag to grab a clean T-shirt. "I'll be there whenever you want to talk or if you have any issues from the kidnapping. We'll be in touch even after I leave Cherry Cove. Sometimes it takes a while to heal from emotional trauma, and things come up later. If you need it, I'll put you in contact with a counselor that can help you more than I can. We have some psychologists that specialize in victims of traumatic events who work with Last Hope and keep our secrets."

"Right now, I just feel exhausted," I told Colin honestly.

"Probably because you haven't slept much in days," he replied. "You need to get some rest, Emma. We can talk more tomorrow. I'll bed down in one of the recliners."

I shook my head. "You don't have to do that. You need to rest, too, and this bed is enormous."

For some reason I really didn't want Colin out of my sight.

"Please?" I added. "I'll feel safer if you're closer."

Now that my body was calming down from the overload of adrenaline, I felt a little vulnerable.

I didn't want to be needy, but I really didn't want to be alone tonight.

"That's pretty normal, Emma," Colin said as he tossed the shirt aside without putting it on. "I'll sleep here if that's what you need."

I let out a sigh of relief as I slid under the covers and put my head on the pillow.

It felt absolutely amazing to actually be in a very comfortable bed again.

I watched as Colin pulled the covers back on his side of the bed.

"You're not going to sleep in your jeans," I commented as he looked like he was about to slide into bed.

"I am," he said hoarsely. "My leg isn't a pretty sight, and I don't inflict that sight on anyone except myself."

"No," I said empathically. "You won't be comfortable. I don't care what your leg looks like. Don't be silly."

He shot me a disgruntled look. "Nobody has ever called me silly."

I didn't doubt that.

Colin was a serious man most of the time, and I was sure he was respected by his peers.

However, he was being silly.

He never used pajamas.

He slept in his underwear or in the raw.

There was no way he was going to sleep well in heavy jeans.

"I don't care what your leg looks like. I want you to sleep comfortably. Take the jeans off."

"Fine," he said in an irritated voice. "I'm turning the light off."

"Don't," I insisted. "I think it's time that you rip off the Band-Aid and let someone see your leg. It's nothing to be ashamed of, Colin. You did something incredibly brave and selfless, and you were injured doing it. It's not something ugly that can't be seen by the people who care about you. I'm definitely not going to judge. I've changed, too."

"Not this much," he grumbled as he finally popped the button on his jeans. "Don't say I didn't warn you."

Watching Colin take off his clothes wasn't new for me, but my breath caught as he kicked out of the denim.

The scarring was significant, and it twisted my heart in my chest as I realized just how much this man had been through because of his injuries.

He was wearing a pair of black boxer briefs. It looked like the scarring probably started on his upper thigh and continued to his ankle. His knee was slightly misshapen, probably due to his many surgeries to try to fix his leg.

Tears filled my eyes, but I blinked them back.

It was a horrible sight, but not for the reasons he imagined.

It killed me to think of how much pain Colin had been through with his injury.

It wasn't ugly.

It was part of Colin now, and there was nothing about this man that could ever be ugly to me.

"Thank you," I said softly as Colin slipped into bed and turned off the light.

"For what?" he said in a defensive voice.

"For letting me be the person you trusted enough to take your pants off," I said sincerely. "Don't be ashamed of those scars. They're part of who you are now. I hate the pain that injury must have put you through for a long time."

"It happened a long time ago, Emma," he said gruffly. "It doesn't hurt anymore. I'm fine."

Ugh! I hated it when Colin acted like an impenetrable fortress that no one could breach.

It had gotten worse than it had been years ago.

At one time, he'd been capable of smiling when he was happy, and he'd been able to let some of those walls down at times.

Now, I doubted he let anyone see the real Colin Marshall.

The only time he'd shown a hint of emotion was when he thought I was uncomfortable in some way.

After his injury, he'd built up those walls brick by brick until no one could see the incredible man he really was.

What in the hell had happened to his teasing and his wicked sense of humor?

I knew that man was still there, but I couldn't quite reach him.

I could sense it.

Colin really hadn't changed. He'd just learned to contain the man he used to be.

He'd always been overly serious, gruff, and contemplative, but he'd taken that to a whole different level.

However, he had put his own life at risk to save me, and I was determined to return the favor by bringing out the parts of Colin that were hidden away from everyone.

"If no one has seen your leg, does that mean you have sex with your clothes on?" I asked jokingly.

"No," he answered roughly.

"In the dark then?" I questioned.

"Not in the dark," he said in a frustrated voice. "I haven't been with a woman since our fling. There isn't a woman on the planet who would want to be close to me after seeing my leg."

Not once?

Not a single female since he and I had been together?

How was that even possible?

I hadn't been with another guy since Colin, either, but it was hard for me to believe he hadn't had sex in fourteen years.

He was a virile man with a *very* healthy sexual appetite.

"Of course women would want to get close to you," I said as I moved until my body was plastered against his and my head was on his chest. "You're a beautiful man, Colin."

God, did he really think his leg would take away from his overall attractiveness?

His entire body stiffened for a moment before it finally relaxed and he wrapped an arm around me protectively.

"You're insane if you really believe that," he rumbled.

"I really believe it, and I'm not crazy," I retorted.

I was still insanely attracted to Colin, just like I'd been years ago.

Yes, I realized that our short relationship had ended a long time ago, and that the attraction couldn't go anywhere, but it was still there.

The truth was, I'd just never felt that kind of attraction again after Colin, which was one of the reasons I'd never been able to be with another man.

I'd tried dating a few times, but none of those first dates had ever turned into a second.

I let out a small sigh as Colin stroked a hand through my hair to comfort me.

"Sleep, Emma," he said soothingly. "You haven't gotten any decent sleep since the kidnapping."

My eyes closed, and I felt a profound sense of peace way down to my soul.

I felt safe here in Colin's arms, and that was something I hadn't felt since the kidnapping.

I was exhausted and worn out, my body totally depleted.

Right now, I felt like I was exactly where I belonged.

I knew I couldn't let myself get used to being this close to Colin, but for right now, while I still felt vulnerable, I was going to revel in it.

For the first time in days, my body completely relaxed.

"That's right," Colin said gently. "Relax and sleep. I'll take care of you, Emma."

"I'm a grown woman," I said sleepily. "It's not your job to take care of me."

"It is my job," he answered in a gruff voice. "I'm your advisor. I'm here to give you whatever you need."

Colin had no idea what my needs were when it came to him. If he did, he wouldn't have just offered to give me *whatever* I needed.

Dammit! I was going to have to get over my intense physical attraction to this man.

That was the last thought that drifted through my mind before I fell into the deep, healing sleep that my body desperately needed.

CHAPTER 12

Marshall

"Now that I'm awake," Emma said after she ate the last of the lemon pastry I'd given her for breakfast. "We really need to talk."

Unfortunately, the only thing I could give her was coffee and that pastry for breakfast because it was the only thing we had on board the aircraft.

I'd feed her something more nutritious later.

She looked a little more rested after getting some decent sleep.

She also looked so beautiful that it was almost painful as she sat on the bed with her mug of coffee and her legs crossed in front of her.

Her hair was slightly tousled. Unfortunately, that made her look even sexier.

The short nightgown she was wearing didn't cover a lot of her fair skin. I wasn't sure whether I was grateful for that or if I hated it.

Hell, I liked looking at Emma this way, but my dick liked it, too, and it wasn't easy to hide my erection since I hadn't bothered to put on my jeans when I'd gone to get her coffee and that pastry.

I'd pulled the bed coverings to my waist when I'd seated myself next to her to drink my coffee.

She'd frowned at me a little, probably because she thought I was trying to cover my scarred leg.

Actually, I wasn't.

She'd seen my leg and she hadn't run away in horror. In fact, she hadn't even flinched when she'd surveyed that injury.

In reality, I was trying to keep the hard-on I'd been sporting since I'd woken up with her voluptuous body sprawled across me hidden from view.

Christ! I wasn't a damn teenager that couldn't control my dick, but I suddenly felt like one because I was in the same room with Emma.

I was in my fifties now for fuck's sake.

I was disgusted with my body's reaction to this woman.

Yeah, she'd shown no aversion to my messed-up leg, but that didn't mean the physical attraction was mutual.

Emma needed me to support her and comfort her right now after her kidnapping, and that was exactly what I was going to do.

Somehow, I was going to have to learn to keep my cock from bouncing to attention every damn time I saw her.

I'd seen plenty of beautiful women in the last fourteen years, and *that* had never happened.

I finally answered Emma, "So, talk. I want you to talk to me, Emma. That's why I'm here as your advisor."

We had about two hours before we'd be landing in Traverse City. We had plenty of time to drink our coffee and talk about whatever was bothering her.

She shook her head slowly as she met my gaze. "I don't want to talk to my advisor and I don't want to talk about the kidnapping. I want to talk to you, Colin."

I shrugged. "Talk about whatever you want."

My gut clenched as I saw the look of trepidation on her face before she said, "I'm just trying to figure out how to say this."

She looked nervous, and I hated it. "Just tell me whatever you have to say. I'm not here to judge you."

"I have a daughter, Colin. Her name is Wren," she blurted out. "She's a huge part of my life that I want to talk about."

Okay, that was a little surprising, but it really wasn't a big deal that she had a child. I hadn't been with another woman for obvious reasons, but Emma hadn't had a reason not to be with other men.

I knew she wasn't with anyone now, but... "Were you married to her father?"

She shook her head. "No."

Fuck! I was going to have to pry information out of her to get her to start talking about her kid, and that was unusual for Emma.

"How old is she?" I asked.

"She's thirteen," Emma answered hesitantly. "Colin, she's not just *my* daughter. She's *your* daughter, too. Wren was conceived during our fling in Virginia Beach. It never should have happened, but it did. I'm sorry. I had no way to contact you to let you know."

I was so fucking stunned that I couldn't utter a single word.

My mind automatically rejected the thought of having a kid.

It wasn't possible, right?

Emma and I had been careful.

We'd had one broken condom incident, but Emma had told me she was safe from pregnancy concerns.

I finally pulled my head out of my ass enough to see that tears were streaming from Emma's beautiful blue eyes.

"I don't want or expect anything from you," she said tearfully. "Wren and I have been fine with just the two of us. I just thought you had a right to know now that I've been able to see you again."

Holy Fuck!

It *was* true.

"How?" I rasped. "I know we had the broken condom incident, but you told me that you couldn't get pregnant."

"I know," she said regretfully. "I shouldn't have gotten pregnant. I was supposedly infertile because of my PCOS, Colin. That's the reason my ex dumped me for another woman with a healthier reproductive system. We tried for years. The only other possible option was artificial insemination for me. My ex-husband didn't want to go that route because it was expensive and there was no guarantee it would result in a child. He decided to just find a woman who could give him the kids he wanted. I wasn't on birth control yet when we met, but I had no reason to think I needed it for protection. Wren was my miracle baby. My gynecologist was surprised, but she said it wasn't totally impossible for me to conceive naturally, but it was extremely unlikely."

It took me a moment to let that information sink into my brain.

It wasn't like I blamed her for getting pregnant.

Emma had good reason to believe she was infertile back then.

My mind was still trying to accept the fact that I had a daughter I hadn't known about for thirteen fucking years.

"Were you upset when you found out?" I finally asked huskily.

"Not upset," she denied. "I was shocked. I knew my entire life was going to change, but I wanted Wren from the moment I found out that I was pregnant. I'd already resigned myself to the fact that I'd probably never have the child I wanted. I consoled myself with the thought that I might be able to adopt someday as a single parent. After I found out, my mother urged me to come home to Cherry Cove so she could be there to support me and help me when I needed it. I relocated back to Michigan before Wren was born and started my own business."

That information sobered me, and I wanted to kick myself for not giving a thought to how difficult this pregnancy must have been for Emma.

She'd been a single parent trying to start up her own business.

She'd been there for our daughter when I hadn't been.

"I should have left you my damn contact information," I said, my voice raw.

"No regrets," Emma said emphatically. "I would have told you if I'd had your contact information, but I didn't. I don't regret it, Colin. Wren has been the joy in my life since the moment she was born. We can't go back and change anything that happened, but please know I'll never regret having our daughter. I wanted you to know the truth, but I don't expect anything from you. Wren is going into high school. She survived her childhood just fine without two parents."

I quickly calculated my daughter's *exact* age.

It hadn't been quite fourteen years since Emma and I had been together.

I frowned. "She has to be *barely* thirteen."

Emma nodded. "We just celebrated her birthday last month. She's been a mini adult since grade school. She has a genius IQ that she definitely didn't inherit from me, but I wouldn't let her skip a grade until she told me she was bored in school. I finally agreed to let her skip her last year of grade school after she begged me to do it. I wish I could show you her picture, but I don't have my phone."

I swallowed the lump in my throat and requested, "Tell me what she looks like."

Emma shrugged. "She looks like you. She has your brown hair and gray eyes. To me, she's the cutest kid on the planet."

Fucking hell!

I still couldn't quite wrap my head around the fact that I had a child in the world that I didn't know, but I was slowly accepting it.

"Who is she staying with while you're gone?"

"She's in San Diego with my mother. That's the only reason I agreed to go to Lania," Emma shared. "She's been spending time with my mom in San Diego in the summer for the last few years. The two of them are really close."

"What does Wren know about me?" I asked.

"As much as I know," Emma told me. "She's always known that I didn't know where you were and it wasn't your fault that you didn't know about her. I told her the whole story about Virginia Beach just recently because she finally asked those questions. I saw no reason not to tell her that we had a fling and that we didn't share any information. I've always tried to be honest with Wren. She's not going to expect anything from you, either, Colin. She knows that you never knew about her."

Everything that I'd missed in Wren's life suddenly hit me.

I hadn't been there for Emma, and I hadn't been there for my daughter all of these years.

"Fuck that!" I said angrily. "She should expect things from me. You should expect things from me. I'm her goddamn father."

"You've known you're a father for a matter of minutes," Emma argued. "What I'm saying is that you don't have to jump in as a father if you don't want to, and we've managed okay financially. I'm not suddenly going to start asking for child support or something."

"I'm going to have to insist that you let me help," I answered tersely. "You've borne the expense of our daughter alone for all these years. That's bullshit."

"She hasn't suffered because she didn't have a father, Colin," Emma said softly.

Yeah, that was probably because Emma had sacrificed everything to give our kid everything she needed.

That was going to end right fucking now.

"I'm not wealthy like my billionaire partners," I informed Emma. "But I'm extremely well-off. I'm more than capable of handling our daughter's expenses and her college expenses in the future."

Emma looked confused. "How is that possible? You're a retired veteran, and Last Hope is a volunteer organization."

Hell, I knew I was going to have to share something with her that I hadn't shared with another soul.

"I'm not retired," I explained. "And I've been investing since the day I got my first paycheck from the military. Those investments have paid off extremely well. I also work for the US government. I'm a contractor on top secret operations. You're the only person I've ever told about my job, and I'd prefer to keep it that way. Most of my work is done by computer, but I get paid well for it."

"Are you a government hacker?" she guessed.

I shrugged. "Maybe. Let's just say I gather intel and I'm exceptionally good at it."

Emma held up a hand. "Okay, I get it. You can't really talk about it, and I'm okay with that. I'm assuming it's highly sensitive information."

"Very sensitive," I confirmed. "Lives depend on me keeping it to myself."

She tilted her head. "Yet you just told me about it."

"We have a child, Emma," I said irritably. "You need to know that I'm not on a budget and unable to provide for Wren now and in the future."

"She's going to want you in her life, Colin," Emma shared. "But she'll understand if that isn't something you're prepared to do. I don't even know if you've ever wanted a child."

An hour ago, I would have said it wasn't something I wanted.

Now that I knew I had a kid in the world, I wasn't sure exactly what I wanted.

Hell yes, now that I knew Wren existed, I wanted to be in her life somehow.

"I'm not just going to walk away," I admitted. "I have no idea how to be a father, Emma. I'm sure I'll suck at it. I've never even interacted much with kids. It wasn't something I ever wanted before, but I sure as fuck can't pretend that Wren doesn't exist."

I wanted to be there for my child. I just wasn't sure *how* to do that.

"She's not a typical kid," Emma said in a warning voice. "She's kind of like a small, very intelligent adult in a teenage body. Her brain functions like an adult, but she still has teenage hormones and emotions. Just get to know her, Colin. She's not going to expect you to instantly be her father. Honestly, she's a lot like you. We'll tell her together when she gets back from San Diego. I'd like to give her some time with her grandmother first if that's okay. Wren has another two weeks there before she comes back to spend the rest of the summer with me. She looks forward to her time with my mom in San Diego every year."

"That works," I agreed. "I think you need some time to recover from the kidnapping, and I don't expect her to change her life just because her father finally decided to show up."

Hell, now that I knew that Wren existed, I wanted to meet her today. But my needs were secondary to what was best for Emma and Wren.

"I'll fill you in on Wren's past before you meet her," Emma promised. "Just tell me what you want to know."

"Start from the moment you knew you were pregnant and fill me in on what happened for the next fourteen years," I requested.

Emma threw her head back and laughed.

Fuck! It was the first time I'd heard her laugh like that in years, and it made my gut twist painfully.

I'd loved her laugh so much that I'd done everything possible to hear it years ago.

"That's going to take more time than we have on this flight," she said once she'd recovered.

"We have time in Cherry Cove," I said with a shrug.

I'd make time to hear about everything I'd missed over the last fourteen years.

For the first time in my life, Last Hope and my work wasn't my priority. I knew in my gut that my regimented life was about to be turned upside down, and I wasn't quite sure how I felt about *that*.

CHAPTER 13

Emma

"We can do a paternity test if you want to know for sure that Wren is your child," I told Colin later that night as we laid in my bed in my beach cottage.

The bed was a queen, so we were cozier than we'd been in the king on the jet, but Colin hadn't complained.

He'd asked if I was ready to be alone, and he'd offered to sleep on the couch.

All I'd had to do was shake my head hesitantly and Colin had removed his jeans and his shirt before he had slipped into the bed beside me without another word.

All Wren and I had ever needed was this two-bedroom cottage, and Wren's bed was smaller than mine. He'd be pretty uncomfortable trying to wedge himself into her shorter bed.

Selfishly, I'd also wanted him to stay close to me.

I'd told him that my captivity had been short, and I didn't think I was going to need a counselor, but I was still edgy from the events that had taken place over those few days I was in Lania.

I knew those feelings would probably go away after I was home for a while, but I really didn't want to be far from Colin, especially at night.

I'd spent the whole day and evening catching him up on absolutely everything about Wren's childhood. He'd asked a lot of questions, and I'd answered every one of them honestly.

Things hadn't always been easy for me as a single mom. Money had been tight at times, especially in the beginning while I was still establishing myself in my own business. But I'd made sure that my daughter had a happy childhood and I'd always done my best to make sure that Wren knew she was loved.

I'd never wanted my mother to pay to raise my daughter, but I'd gratefully let her babysit for free when I needed to work. I'd also let her spoil her only grandchild shamelessly.

"Not necessary," Colin said as he wrapped his arm around me and tugged me closer to him. "She looks too much like me not to be my child. I know she's my daughter."

We'd spent some time during the evening going through my picture albums, so he'd seen his daughter at all different ages.

"I've never been with anyone else since you, Colin," I blurted out. "It would be impossible for me to have a child with anyone but you. I was really focused on just being Wren's mom, and I've never met anyone else that I wanted to be with intimately."

His arm tightened around me harder, and I snuggled against his big, warm, burly body.

"How is that possible?" he asked huskily. "You must have men falling at your feet. You're a beautiful woman, Emma."

I snorted. "I was a single, curvy mom who talked about little else except her child. Unless I had a video meeting with a client, I didn't even bother to put on makeup. That's not the least bit attractive."

Colin was crazy if he thought that men had fallen at my feet.

Even if that was true, which it definitely wasn't, my heart had just never been into dating.

"You're still the most beautiful woman I've ever seen," Colin said unhappily. "The men in Michigan must be idiots if they didn't see that."

My heart tripped. Did he really believe that?

"I've gained weight—"

"You're curvy in all the right places," he interrupted.

I let out a sound of disgust. "I'm forty-five, and I'm starting to see wrinkles on my face."

"That means you have some life experience," he stated. "Also attractive."

I let out a sigh of resignation. "You're impossible. You're probably the only guy who thinks those tiny wrinkles are attractive."

"We've both gotten older, Emma," he said stoically.

"Men get more attractive as they age," I argued. "Women just get…old."

"I definitely didn't," he grumbled.

"You did," I protested. "It's annoying. You're still as ruggedly handsome as you were fourteen years ago. You're ridiculously fit. You really haven't changed much."

"My leg is a mess," he rumbled.

"Which doesn't make one bit of a difference on the attractiveness scale," I blurted out before I could think about my words. "I still think you're the hottest man on the planet. It's annoying. You've gotten even hotter and I'm just getting old and plump."

"You still think I'm attractive?' he asked, sounding perplexed.

"Ridiculously attractive," I answered honestly. I'd gone too far not to be completely truthful. "I'm just as attracted to you as I was fourteen years ago. I know that can never go anywhere. Our fling was a long time ago, and it's been over for a long time. That's crazy, right?"

"Not so crazy," he said hoarsely. "I'm still attracted to you, too. But you've been through a lot of trauma, and I'm familiar to you. Once you feel more secure, that attraction is likely to change for you."

Ha! I was a mature adult, and I knew my emotions. Wanting to get Colin naked was not going to change for *me*.

Did he really think that his previously injured leg mattered to me?

He might be more guarded and a little edgier than he had been fourteen years ago, but he was exactly the same man he was years ago.

And that man had turned me inside out.

It was no different now.

Maybe I shouldn't have blurted out the fact that I still thought he was scorching hot, but Colin and I had always been honest with each other.

The fact that he still found me desirable was something I hadn't expected, but it made me feel less vulnerable knowing that I wasn't alone in those feelings that had never quite gone away.

"It's not going to change," I said bluntly. "But I'll learn to live with it. I want the two of us to be friends. We have a daughter, and I want us to be comfortable with each other again."

"I'm not the same man I was years ago," he said in a warning voice.

Yes, he was. He'd just gotten good at hiding the old Colin beneath a humorless, stoic façade that I wasn't buying for a single moment.

His injury had made him build up a ton of defenses to push people away.

That made sense because his injury had changed his life profoundly, and he'd tried to make himself invulnerable.

It wasn't like Colin had ever been a warm and fuzzy guy, but he'd been able to let people in once he got to know and trust them.

Honestly, I wasn't sure if he'd let anyone see the real Colin in years.

To me, that was incredibly sad because deep down there was a part of him that was very real and very human.

He also had a heart-stopping smile when he chose to utilize it.

I sat up a little and rested my head on my hand as I looked at him.

The moonlight coming from the window of my bedroom wouldn't allow me to see his face clearly, but I'd felt his body tense up. "You're exactly the same," I informed him. "You just hide the person you are better than you used to."

"You're wrong," he ground out in an irritated voice.

"I don't believe you," I said persistently. "You risked your life to save mine. You didn't have to do that."

"That doesn't mean I'm not still an asshole," he said in an annoyed tone. "It was a calculated risk."

God, he was so full of shit, but I'd let him get away with it…for now. He'd built up those defenses for years.

It would take time for him to let go of some of them.

"Have I thanked you for coming to Lania and for everything you've done for me?" I asked him.

"Yes," he said abruptly. "Don't thank me, Emma. Rescuing hostages is what I do, and you're the mother of my child."

I smiled into the darkness.

He hadn't known I was the mother of his child when he'd come for me, and he operated Last Hope out of the headquarters in San Diego. He ran missions, but he wasn't usually a participant in the actual recovery.

I knew he'd involved himself in my rescue because he knew me and it was somehow personal to him. Maybe it had been years since we'd seen each other, but he'd still felt some sense of obligation to rescue me himself.

That was the Colin I'd known and adored.

The man with a big heart that he rarely showed to anyone.

He hadn't changed a bit.

He'd just convinced himself that he had, and that he was a totally humorless asshole without the same heart.

"I'm still going to thank you," I said lightly. "You saved my life."

"I guess I forgot how damn stubborn you can be," he said unhappily.

"You used to like that about me," I teased.

"Fuck!" he cursed as he wrapped his arms around me and rolled on top of me. "I think I still do, but I shouldn't."

My breath caught and my body instantly responded to the feel of his warm, massive body intimately connected to mine.

I was wearing a summer nightgown, and all of that skin-to-skin contact with Colin made my heart skip a beat.

God, he still felt so good.

He still smelled so deliciously incredible.

I automatically wrapped my arms around his neck to get even closer to him.

My body still craved him like an addictive drug, and it was a temptation that was too difficult to ignore.

"Kiss me," I whispered before I could stop those words from escaping my lips. "Please. Just once."

It would be a stupid thing to do, but at the moment, I didn't care.

I was feeling things I hadn't felt for fourteen long years, and I wanted to feel the way I had with Colin all those years ago.

I'd been so consumed with being a mother and with building my career that I'd forgotten what it felt like to just be a woman with the normal desires of a female.

I wanted to remember.

Just for a moment.

Colin hesitated for a moment, but an instant later he lowered his head and captured my lips in an embrace that rocked my entire world.

He was a man that did nothing without throwing himself into whatever he did wholeheartedly.

His kiss was no different.

He devoured my mouth like it was his only mission in life, and I reveled in that passion.

Colin explored my mouth with a thoroughness that took my breath away, like it was the first time he'd ever touched me this way.

Greedily.

And with a slight desperation that made my heart soar.

He still wanted me as much as I wanted him, and that knowledge made me respond with wanton recklessness that I didn't think was even possible for me anymore.

I didn't think.

I just allowed myself to feel every emotion his kiss rang out of me.

It had only ever been this way with him.

Only with Colin.

I felt like I was the most desirable woman in the world.

And didn't want to waste a nanosecond of those sensations.

I knew it wouldn't last.

I knew we couldn't turn back the clock and rekindle what we'd had fourteen years ago.

Years ago, we'd been completely focused on mind-blowing sex.

I couldn't say that the carnality wasn't still there, but now there was something…more.

My hands roamed over his back as he consumed my mouth because all I wanted to do was explore this man all over again.

Colin abruptly lifted his head and I let out a little moan of protest. "Fucking hell, Emma!" he spat out. "We can't do this. You're still vulnerable and I'm pawing you like a horny teenager."

He rolled onto his back, wrapped an arm around me, and pulled me close to him.

I was still panting as I put my head on his shoulder. "I wasn't exactly complaining. I asked you to kiss me."

"That doesn't mean I should have done it," he said in a graveled voice. "I'm your advisor. I should have known better. You probably have no idea what you want right now."

Oh, I'd known exactly what I'd wanted.

Yes, I was vulnerable, but I always had been when it came to him.

"I knew that I wanted you to kiss me," I said empathetically.

I wasn't going to let him think he took advantage of me in a vulnerable position.

That would be complete and utter crap.

"We'll chalk this up to temporary insanity and lack of sleep for both of us," he decided. "It won't happen again."

I let out a long sigh.

It probably couldn't happen again.

I was a forty-five-year-old mom to a teenage daughter.

It wasn't like I could indulge in another fling with the father of my child.

Honestly, I probably wasn't capable of having another fling with Colin.

Although I didn't regret what had happened, the last one had broken my heart.

I was going to have to get over the lingering attraction I had to Colin and focus on the fact that we were Wren's parents together and nothing more.

Maybe remembering I was a woman with my own needs hadn't been such a great idea after all.

CHAPTER 14

Marshall

"You don't have to tell me that Wren is your kid," Brock stated as I opened the door the next morning.

Emma had run to the store because she'd emptied everything perishable out of her refrigerator before she'd left for Lania.

I'd been working in the living room until the knock on the door of the cottage.

I watched as Brock, Nate, Gage, and Seth strode into Emma's place like they knew it well, which they probably did.

There was an enormous painting that I knew Nate had done for Emma in her living room, and pictures of the men everywhere.

I wasn't sure why it irritated me just a little that these men had been part of Emma and Wren's life before I'd ever known that Wren existed.

"Make yourself comfortable," I said drily as the men did exactly that.

Nate, Gage, and Seth flopped onto the large sofa while Brock took the recliner next to the one I'd been occupying.

The cottage was small, and the door basically led directly into the living room.

There was a small dining table in the space between the kitchen and the living room.

The hallway led to the bedrooms and a full bathroom.

Emma had laughingly told me yesterday that she was glad she had her own bathroom attached to her bedroom so she didn't have to share a bathroom with a teenager.

Emma's house and my place in San Diego couldn't be more different.

Although the cottage was clean, it was cluttered with pictures of everyone she knew and loved.

It also held a lot of mementos of Wren's childhood and things Emma and Wren had done together.

She had all of her history in this cottage, and Emma had never been a woman where everything had a specific place.

I was a minimalist who had almost nothing personal in my home.

I was also anal about everything having a specific place. My neatness was probably a remnant of my military career.

I hated clutter.

Emma, however, seemed to wallow in it.

Strangely, it was an endearing habit of hers that had never really bothered me.

When we'd been at the beach house years ago, I'd happily just picked up the things she'd dropped to put away later.

I closed the door and seated myself back in my recliner.

"How did you know that Wren was my child?" I asked Brock.

"I knew it the minute you said that you and Emma had met fourteen years ago. We've all known that Emma had no way to contact Wren's father because it was a Virginia Beach fling. Wren looks just like you. She's also always reminded me of someone, but I couldn't put a finger on who it was until that moment. She has your genius IQ and she's serious for a kid her age."

I looked at the four men, and their expressions were all somber.

I'd been working with them closely for years, but I knew very little about their personal lives.

It wasn't completely comfortable for me to be talking to them about personal subjects even though I'd known them for a long time.

"No offense intended," Seth said grimly. "But Emma and Wren are important in our lives. I guess we'd kind of like to know your intentions now that you do know about Wren."

I grimaced. It was really none of their damn business what my intentions were. I answered to no one.

However, I stifled the instinct to tell them any of those thoughts. Brock, Nate, Gage, and Seth had been there for Emma and Wren. They'd looked out for their best interests when I couldn't.

I could hardly fault them for watching out for Emma and my daughter.

Hell, I appreciated it even though it irked me that I hadn't been part of Emma and my daughter's lives until now.

"I didn't know about Wren until yesterday," I said stiffly. "I intend to get to know her as soon as possible. I'm going to be part of her life in every way possible now that I do know. Hopefully with emotional support as well as financial. As you probably already know, I'm not sure exactly how to emotionally support my daughter, but I'll figure it out."

"She's a hard kid not to like," Gage mused. "She's a normal girl in some ways, and like a small adult in others. She's way too smart for her age, and really good with computers just like you. I think she's always wanted to fit in with girls her age, but she's always felt a little different because of her intelligence level."

I could actually relate to that. I never quite fit in with kids my age when I was younger, either.

Hell, I wasn't exactly social with most people *now*.

"I get that," I admitted. "I felt the same way when I was younger."

"For what it's worth," Nate added. "I think you'll understand each other in ways others can't. You'll connect with her, Marshall. Just don't hurt her and we won't have to hurt you. I don't think any of us would like that since we respect you."

Okay, I did admire the way these men had looked after Emma and Wren, but enough was enough.

I glared at them. "Do you really think I'd hurt my own daughter?"

"I'm not sure we know you well enough personally to judge," Gage said earnestly. "You've always been all business all the time. That won't work with a girl like Wren."

Gage was right. That was exactly who I was, and I knew that wasn't going to fly with a thirteen-year-old girl.

Christ! Just the thought of figuring out how to have an emotional connection with anyone was daunting, much less trying to figure out how to be a parent to a daughter.

"I have no fucking idea how to be a father," I admitted before I could stop myself. "I never planned on having a child. But I'm not walking away from my daughter now that I know that she exists."

Nate grinned. "We thought we were tough guys, too, until we met Wren. None of us had much interaction with kids, either. She'll get to you. All you have to do is let her in and care about her."

I didn't let anyone in, and I liked it that way. That was the problem.

"All of you know that's just not my personality," I grumbled.

"I think that's bullshit," Brock answered. "You care about people, Marshall. You wouldn't be doing what you do with Last Hope if you didn't. We know what you did for Wyatt when Shelby's life was in danger. We also know you didn't have to give yourself up for Emma and put your own ass on the line. I very much doubt you'd ever hurt anyone intentionally. But you're going to have to drop some of your defenses to get to know Wren. She's a kid. She's not going to understand that you care if you never show it."

"I'll figure it out," I answered in a voice that would let them know that I was about done talking about this subject.

They all nodded.

"I think you will figure it out," Gage said. "You're staying for a while?"

"I am," I replied brusquely.

"How long?" Seth questioned.

"As long as it takes to get to know my daughter when she gets back from San Diego. I talked to Wyatt this morning. Until further notice, he and the rest of my partners there will be handling Last Hope operations." I glanced at Brock. "If you suspected that Wren was my daughter, why didn't you mention her before I left for Lania?"

He shrugged. "It wasn't my place to make that call or to tell you about my suspicions. That was a decision that Emma needed to make. She's her mom."

I found it interesting that Wyatt had said the same when I'd talked to him this morning. He'd suspected the same thing but hadn't wanted to make any assumptions or step on Emma's toes.

Hell, even Wyatt had met my daughter several times in the past.

"What about Emma?" Nate asked cautiously.

I lifted a brow. "What about her?"

"We think she still has feelings for you," Seth clarified. "We've always thought so. Through the years, she's clutched that pendant you gave her like it's her lifeline, and she's never shown any real interest in another guy. She's never admitted it, but I think it broke her heart when you left her without saying goodbye."

Okay, so these men obviously knew a lot about my short history with Emma.

That didn't surprise me since Emma was my total opposite. She probably talked about things with the people she cared about.

She was open, genuine, and honest with people.

I...wasn't.

"It was fourteen years ago," I said gruffly.

Yeah, there had been that idiotic kiss the night before, but I was convinced that Emma had just needed some kind of comfort from me. She'd been one day out from her trauma of the kidnapping.

That kiss had been familiar to her.

For me, it had been too damn familiar.

It didn't seem like it was even possible that I probably wanted her more today than I had fourteen years ago.

But...I did.

And I hated myself for not having enough control to back off Emma when she was vulnerable.

I'd made myself her damn advisor. I was supposed to be looking out for her best interests right now.

Kissing her had been a selfish, dick move on my part.

I should have had the self-discipline to do what was best for *her*.

"Does that really matter?" Nate asked. "Feelings are feelings. You must still care about her, Marshall. You risked your life for hers by surrendering yourself to find her."

"I'm not the same man that I was fourteen years ago," I said harshly. "Do you really think she'd want the man I am today? I'm older and my leg is a mess. You all put yourselves on the line regularly for Last Hope. It shouldn't be surprising that I was willing to do the same thing."

"It's what we've always done," Brock said nonchalantly. "No offense, but you were an officer in command of your missions. It's been a long time since you were actually an operative. I know you were a commander that always insisted on being with your men, but you were in charge of operations. It was our job to carry out those missions." He hesitated for a moment before he added, "I don't think Emma gives a damn about your leg. You're still the same guy she cared about years ago, and none of us wants to see her get her heart broken again. Emma's been like an older sister to all of us for years. We care about her, Marshall."

"I care about her, too, dammit!" I rasped before I could think about my words. "And I'm not capable of breaking her heart. I'm a fifty-three-year-old man who couldn't run if my life depended on it. Emma is young and still just as beautiful as she was fourteen years ago. It's ridiculous to think she'd want a guy like me."

I looked around the living room to see a satisfied look on every one of the men's faces.

Fuck! What in the hell was wrong with these guys?

My thoughts were interrupted as Emma opened the front door and swept into the living room carrying a large grocery bag.

I felt like I took a gigantic gut punch as her face lit up in a smile as she looked at Brock, Nate, Gage, and Seth.

"You're here!" she said excitedly as she dropped the bag. "I saw your cars out front."

The men all stood as Emma entered the room.

Something gnawed at my gut as she threw herself into Brock's arms and then hugged every other man in the room…except me.

Hell, I should be glad she was having an emotional reunion with the men who had watched out for her for years.

However, what was eating at my gut at the moment definitely wasn't *gratitude*.

In fact, it felt suspiciously like an emotion I almost never experienced.

Was it possible that I was actually feeling some kind of…jealousy?

Nah. Not possible.

But as she finished hugging her friends and tossed herself into my arms in an affectionate greeting, I held her tightly, finally admitting to myself that I just *might* have a few possessive emotions toward Emma after all.

It didn't make sense, and I was a man who believed that everything should be rational.

I closed my eyes and held Emma intimately against me for far longer than I should have.

This woman was starting to make me feel irrational, and I wasn't sure I liked feeling those emotions…at all.

CHAPTER 15

Emma

"It's hot," I informed Colin two days later. "Let's take a swim before we barbecue."

Brock, Nate, Gage, and Seth had snagged a picnic table and one of the permanent barbecue grills near the entrance while Colin and I had found a spot on the sandy beach to spread out a bunch of blankets.

It was summer, and the local beach was pretty crowded. Cherry Cove swelled to capacity during the summer because it was a popular beach town.

I'd spent the last two days showing Colin around Cherry Cove.

We'd strolled the shops in town, had ice cream at the well-known, iconic ice cream shop, and we'd all had dinner together at Gage's restaurant, The Beachfront Café, last night.

Little by little, I was starting to feel secure and normal again after my experience in Lania.

Colin still slept in my bed every night, but now it was simply because I wanted to be close to him, not because I felt nervous about being alone.

He'd kept his distance after that incredible kiss, making sure he kept busy.

He'd insisted on mowing my lawn and doing some yard work even though I'd protested.

He'd also fixed anything that wasn't functioning optimally in my cottage, things I just hadn't gotten around to getting fixed yet.

We both worked in the mornings on our computers, but I had a sneaking suspicion that Colin had no idea what to do when he wasn't busy with some kind of work.

The man had no idea how to just relax or how to just spend time with friends doing something for fun.

"I don't swim in public," he informed me stiffly as he dropped the bags he'd carried down to the beach.

I knew he was still self-conscious about his leg, but he really needed to get over that.

He'd purchased a pair of board shorts at my insistence when we were at the shops in town, grumbling because he said he didn't need them.

He was wearing them beneath the jeans and T-shirt he was wearing.

I finished spreading the blankets out and put my hands on my hips. I couldn't really see his eyes beneath the sunglasses he was wearing, but I still glared at him. "Don't be silly," I said firmly. "If I can bare my plump body to swim, you can swim with me."

"Nobody calls me silly," he reminded me.

"Then stop doing silly things," I insisted. "Look around you, Colin. Do you see a bunch of perfect bodies? I'm not sure how things are in California, but nobody here cares if your body isn't perfect. Our summers are short, and all Michiganders want to do is enjoy the summer we have. Let's swim."

He was silent for a moment and I held my breath.

"Go swim," Brock insisted as the guys arrived at our spot. "We'll give you some time before we start getting things ready to go on the grill."

I looked at the men gratefully.

All of them were dressed in swim trunks and a T-shirt.

A few female heads had turned admiring glances their way when the four of them had jogged down to the beach.

I was used to that.

The four of them together were a breathtaking sight to some women.

There wasn't a single one of them that didn't have a ripped body and handsome faces that drew female eyes wherever they went.

Seth was the only blonde, and he had a few scars that nobody seemed to notice except him.

I suppose they were all stunningly gorgeous, but I'd never seen them as anything other than sometimes annoying but beloved younger brother figures.

I adored every one of them, but they fussed a little too much about my safety sometimes.

I indulged them because I knew they only did it because they considered me a close friend.

Honestly, I was grateful that they'd cared enough to insist that I check in every day from Lania.

If they hadn't, it may have taken longer for them to realize that I was missing.

I took a deep breath and lifted my sundress over my head.

Honestly, I wasn't all that brave about revealing my older and plumper body to Colin.

He'd seen me when I was a lot thinner, and at one of the few times in my life when I'd actually looked decent in a bikini.

I was nervous, but I was determined to bring this man out of his shell.

I folded my sundress and dropped it onto the blanket.

There was no way I was stuffing my body into a bikini anymore. The modest one-piece was revealing enough for the forty-five-year-old and heavier me.

It felt weird for me to be self-conscious. I'd accepted who I was and how I looked a long time ago. As long as I was healthy, my fuller body had never really bothered me. I did have PCOS and being at a low weight just wasn't sustainable for me. I liked food far too much to starve myself into a thinner body. I exercised and stayed as fit as I could be. I'd always been content with that.

But that was before I was standing in front of Colin, a man who was used to me having a lighter, more attractive body and a more youthful appearance.

I swallowed hard and consoled myself with the fact that he couldn't see the faded stretch marks on my belly from carrying our daughter.

I watched, my body tense as he took off his sunglasses and dropped them onto the blanket.

His gaze met mine before he pulled the T-shirt over his head and dropped that too.

My heart skittered as my eyes roamed over his muscular chest and abs.

Seriously, how was it possible that he still looked as fit as he had when he was in the military?

He really hadn't changed much.

He still wore his hair military short, and he'd shaved the scruff off his face that he'd gotten from our time in Lania.

The man was ridiculously gorgeous.

Ruggedly handsome.

And stupidly hot for a man his age.

Relief flooded through my body when he shucked his jeans with no fanfare and dropped them beside his T-shirt.

He lifted a brow as he said, "Let's swim."

He took my hand and tugged me toward the water.

Honestly, you couldn't see much of his leg because the board shorts were long, but it wouldn't have mattered if it was completely revealed.

Colin was such an imposing male figure that those scars were hardly even noticeable.

He released my hand as we waded into the water, and I watched in awe as he dove into the depths of Lake Michigan.

Colin had been a SEAL, and he swam like a fish.

He was more comfortable in the water than any other person I'd ever known.

I dove after him.

I'd grown up here in Cherry Cove, and I didn't remember a time when I hadn't been able to swim.

We swam silently for a while, both of us getting our exercise and wearing ourselves out.

When I was totally exhausted, I finally put my feet down in one of the shallow areas that existed from the shifting sands in the protected cove.

The water was nearly up to my chest, but I was able to rest.

I simply watched Colin continue to swim like he was capable of keeping up his rapid pace forever.

I knew he had an eye out for other swimmers in his path, but most of the recreational swimmers were closer to shore.

I was leisurely floating on my back when he finally joined me.

"You're going to get sunburned," he warned as he stood on the sand beside me.

I smiled at him as I put my feet back on the ground. "Not happening. I slathered myself with sunscreen before I left the house."

My skin was fair, and I knew better than to go without sunscreen on a day like this.

Michigan winters were long and brutal, and I didn't get outdoors much when the weather was frigid and the snow was flying.

On the other hand, Colin tanned easily, and he was probably always tanned like he was now from living in California.

He'd mentioned that he swam in his outdoor pool year-round in San Diego.

"I guess we should get back to shore and help with the barbecue," I told him, feeling a little awkward for the first time in Colin's presence.

Maybe I still wasn't quite used to Colin's standoffishness with me.

When we'd been in the water in Virginia Beach, we'd touched each other constantly when we were swimming and we'd played like we were teenagers who were crazy about each other.

"Wait," he demanded as he wrapped an arm around my waist before I could swim away. "You were nervous on the beach. Explain that to me."

Ugh! He'd noticed. Maybe I should have expected that. Colin was the kind of guy who picked up on every nuance of human behavior.

By the time we'd left Virginia Beach, he'd been able to pick up on every one of my emotions.

That had been a little unnerving at first, but I'd gotten used to it.

He might be a man of few words himself, but he was incredibly observant when it came to other people's behavior.

I put my hand on his shoulder to keep my balance as I answered, "Do you really think it was easy for me to bare my body in front of a man who hasn't seen me since I was younger and thinner?"

He tipped my chin up a little so our eyes met. "Yet you had no problem challenging me," he observed.

It *had* been a challenge, and I'd been banking on the fact that Colin never backed down from a challenge.

I shrugged. "Someone needs to do it. I don't think it happens very often. You love to swim. I needed to get you into the water somehow. I wanted to prove to you that nobody cares about your leg. The rest of you is so stupidly perfect that it just doesn't matter."

Then...it suddenly happened, that something that I'd been hoping for since the moment we'd seen each other again.

Colin moved a strand of wet hair from my face and shot me a small grin.

My heart turned over and completely melted.

The man was devastatingly handsome when he was serious and stoic.

When he smiled, he was utterly and deliciously irresistible.

"You always were a bold woman," he told me teasingly. "Nobody challenges me, Emma. Not for a very long time. I think the last time it happened was fourteen years ago when we were in Virginia Beach. You knew damn well that you were going to get me into the water with that challenge."

"It wasn't easy for me," I confessed as I fell into his mesmerizing eyes. "I look a lot different than I did fourteen years ago."

His expression sobered. "Yeah," he conceded. "You look even better than you did back then. Christ, Emma! Do you honestly believe that you're any less attractive than you were when we first met? You're curvier, but those curves look good on you. You were a little too thin when we met. You look healthy and sexier than ever. I had to get into the water. My dick was so hard that I needed to dive into some cold water before anyone noticed."

My heart squeezed hard inside my chest.

Was he just saying that to make me feel better, or did he really believe that?

I asked him that question directly because I wanted to know.

"Have I ever told you anything that wasn't true?" he questioned as he wrapped both of his arms around my waist. "You know I'm not the kind of man who says something just to charm a female."

That was definitely true.

Colin wasn't a natural charmer, but I'd always adored that about him.

What he said was always blunt and honest.

I'd never needed to try to figure out exactly what he meant beneath a bunch of charming words that meant nothing.

I put my arms around his neck to keep my balance as he pulled me closer to him. "I'm really not the kind of woman who inspires lust in any guy. Not at my age with this body," I said honestly.

"You do more than inspire it in *this* guy," he said huskily. "I'm not going to bullshit you Emma because I never have. You're the first woman who has gotten my cock hard since those days we spent together at Virginia Beach. That hasn't changed for me. I hate it, but it's the truth. You're a beautiful woman. But I know I'm going to have to learn to live with that reaction every time I see you."

I rested my head on his shoulder with a long sigh. He was completely serious, and I knew he was being truthful. "I feel the same way. I think I'm always going to be attracted to you, Colin, and I haven't felt this kind of chemistry with a man since we met, either. I know there's nothing I can do about it. I'd like to think it will go away, but I'd be lying to myself. It's not like we can have another fling. We live different lives in different states. We're different people than we were years ago. But it totally sucks that I want to touch you every time I see you."

"How in the hell is that even possible, Emma?" he asked hoarsely. "I'm fifty-three years old and I have a bum leg now. I'm sure you've met men who are whole and attractive."

"You're still whole," I protested as I pulled back to look at his face, completely annoyed with Colin because he didn't know just how attractive he was. "And irritatingly gorgeous. Do you really think I want to be attracted to you? I can't help it. It is what it is. If I could control it, I would. We have a daughter. I'd like the two of us to be friends. I think we can, but I'm always going to want to get you naked. That's really not comfortable for me, either."

That stunning grin formed on his face again, and it made my heart soar all over again.

"Have I ever told you that you're adorable when you're angry?" he asked jokingly.

"This isn't amusing for me," I scolded him. "I'm a forty-five-year-old mom to a teenage daughter and I'm *still* lusting after her father that I haven't seen in fourteen years."

"Hate me for it if you want," he said drily. "But it feels kind of good that you're still attracted to me. When you asked me to kiss you, I thought that you were confused. I'm still just a man, Emma, and I like the fact that you still look at me like you can't wait to get me naked."

I dropped my head to his shoulder again in defeat. "Dammit!" I cursed. "I'm a woman and I like the fact that you still find me attractive, too. I think we're both screwed."

Colin actually let out a small chuckle as his arms tightened around me reflexively.

He'd almost laughed, which made him even more attractive.

God, if this man got any more appealing, I had no idea what I was going to do.

CHAPTER 16

Marshall

"You still care about Emma," Brock stated as we sat on Emma's small deck a few days later.

Everyone else was in the house watching a movie that Brock and I had already seen, so the two of us had stepped out onto the back deck to have a beer.

The patio was only big enough for a few lounge chairs and a side table in between, but it was a peaceful place to be, especially when it was cooler in the evening.

It was warm, but the lake breeze made it comfortable. It wasn't possible to actually see the water from Emma's place, but every location in Cherry Cove experienced the wind coming off Lake Michigan.

I took a swig from my beer as I lounged in the chair next to Brock's.

In the last few days, I'd gotten to know my Michigan team a little better.

I'd discovered that they spent a lot of time with Emma whenever possible.

One or more of them stopped by daily to check on her.

She also had running text messages where she chatted with her friends and her mom throughout the day.

That had seemed a little odd for me at first. I texted people when it regarded something about Last Hope, but I wasn't a phone person.

It had taken a while for me to realize that keeping in touch with the people in her life was something that Emma needed to feel normal.

She was social.

I definitely was…not.

Tonight, Nate had called and suggested they hang out and watch a movie.

Apparently, that was an almost weekly event for all of them.

All four of the guys had arrived earlier with Emma's best friend, Sara, only a few minutes behind them.

I had absolutely no idea what it was like to just hang out with friends for no real practical reason, but I was getting used to Emma's friends dropping by just because they wanted to be with her.

Honestly, I *could* comprehend exactly why people sought out Emma's company.

I was actually pretty motivated to see her beautiful smile as often as possible myself.

I was getting to know Brock pretty well because he dropped by every single day because his writing schedule was fairly flexible.

Those initial feelings of jealousy I'd experienced had faded since the men acted like family to Emma even though they weren't related by blood.

Okay, I still wasn't exactly thrilled when Emma threw herself into their arms, but that was probably because I didn't like to see *any* man touch her.

"What makes you say that?" I asked.

"Come on, Marshall," Brock said impatiently. "You two look at each other like you're crazy about each other. I know Emma. She still has feelings for you. I've never seen her look at anyone else that way. You might be a little more guarded, but you're taking care of her like a guy who cares about her. You've replaced everything in her cottage that needs replacing, and you've bought her more gifts than she can handle." He waved his hand toward the lawn. "Her yard looks like a picture out of a magazine it's so perfect. I think that's your way of showing her that you care because you're not a demonstrative kind of guy. And you two looked pretty cozy in the water at the beach a few days ago."

Brock and I were getting a little more open with each other, so I saw no reason to not share a little bit more. "I'm not sure I ever *stopped* caring," I admitted. "Emma was more than a fling to me fourteen years ago. She was special to me. The timing was all wrong. I was a SEAL commander and I avoided any and all relationships. At the end, I struggled with not exchanging contact information. I wanted to, but I didn't think it was fair to her. She was an incredible woman and a lot younger than I was. I couldn't offer her much. I was always gone or always involved in my responsibilities. I thought she deserved better than whatever I could offer. In hindsight, I should have made sure she knew how to contact me before I left. I went back to the beach house later that morning after I came to my senses, but she was already gone."

"So you wanted a relationship with her?" Brock questioned.

"Selfishly, yes. But I eventually convinced myself that the way we parted was for the best. I was injured on duty shortly after I met her. She would have ended up with a boyfriend that was in and out of the hospital and a total asshole."

Brock shook his head. "You wouldn't have been an asshole to her. She was pregnant, remember? And she would have been by your side throughout your entire recovery. That recovery period would have looked a lot different for you with her by your side. What do you want from Emma now?"

I thought about that for a minute.

Hell, things probably would have been different.

Brock was right.

I would have been thinking more about Emma and our child rather than being a selfish asshole feeling sorry for myself because my career was over.

I could have also been there to help her financially in the beginning when things were tough for her and Wren.

I *should* have been there and leaving that beach house in Virginia Beach without leaving my number had been a monumental mistake that I now regretted. Maybe I had felt like I was doing the right thing at the time, but I should have said to hell with our deal and left my damn number.

What did I want from Emma now?

"Nothing?" I answered roughly. "I can't expect or want anything from Emma. She raised our daughter on her own. Her life is here in Cherry Cove with Wren. Eventually, I have to go back to San Diego. I can't leave Wyatt and the other guys in charge of headquarters forever. They have wives and a work life. They didn't sign up for that."

Brock shrugged. "All relationships take some compromises. If things work out, I'm not sure Emma would mind moving to San Diego. Her mom is there, and Wren loves it there. It's an expensive place for a single parent, but you two could work something out."

And if things didn't work out?

Hell, I didn't even want to consider that possibility.

It was a lot safer not to take that risk in the first place.

Emma and I had always had intense chemistry, but a relationship was something else entirely.

I'd never had a long-term relationship.

It was very likely that I'd fail at being a real partner to someone.

I sucked at showing any kind of emotion, and Emma needed a guy who would cherish her the right way.

"You're giving a lot of advice for a single guy who doesn't have any entanglements himself," I grumbled.

Brock grinned. "I'm about to turn forty. If I haven't found a woman who can put up with me by now, I never will. I was Delta. I avoided relationships for the same reasons you did when you were in the military. Now, I have Last Hope and I disappear at a moment's notice. I also travel when I need to for book events. Maybe I'm getting set in my ways. I like the way my life is right now."

Did he?

Or had he sacrificed his own personal life for Last Hope?

The whole Michigan team was extremely active in Last Hope.

Maybe I'd never stopped to wonder if they were giving up too much to be the primary operating team for the volunteer rescue operation. "Are you avoiding relationships because of Last Hope?"

"Nah," Brock denied. "It's not like there aren't married guys involved in Last Hope. Honestly, I prefer to be single."

I frowned at him. He was probably being truthful. Most likely, he'd never met a woman he wanted more than his freedom.

"It's probably none of my business," I said. "But I noticed that none of you seem to be suffering financially from giving a lot of your time to Last Hope. I know that your career is lucrative, but I'm curious."

All four of the men had extremely nice homes with a lake view that were in fairly close proximity to each other.

Nice vehicles.

And very nice toys that most normal guys couldn't afford.

Brock chuckled. "Are you kidding? We're close to Wyatt Durand. He made damn sure our financial future was secure from day one in Delta. None of us spent much of our paychecks in the military because we were always gone. He started a portfolio for all of us and invested those funds for all of the years we were in Delta. He taught us how to secure our futures. Up until a few years ago, he gifted us stocks for our birthdays and the holidays. We finally had to put our feet down a few years ago and make him stop. We were all skilled investors ourselves by that time, and we had good careers. We were perfectly capable of continuing to invest on our own. He wasn't happy, but he was content with the knowledge that we could all retire tomorrow and never hurt for money for the rest of our lives. We all make a good living. We aren't billionaires like Wyatt, but money really isn't a concern for any of us."

Hell, I probably should have known that Wyatt would make sure his guys never hurt for money. He'd been a billionaire with savvy financial skills before he'd gone into Delta, so he'd had those investment and financial skills to share with his men.

I was glad that Wyatt had made it his business to make sure our Michigan team was financially secure. None of them got paid for their involvement in Last Hope, but they dedicated a significant amount of their time and energy to the organization.

Last Hope's success probably meant as much to these guys as it did to the headquarters team.

I'd picked Wyatt's brain many times myself on investments, and his advice had allowed my net worth to grow even larger over time.

"Something tells me that Wyatt shared his financial advice with you, too," Brock said like he'd just read my mind.

I nodded. "I started investing as soon as I got into the military just like you did. I didn't need most of my paycheck, either. But Wyatt's advice has been invaluable over the years. I don't have financial worries. I'm more than capable of taking care of anything Emma and Wren need in the future."

Yeah, I was getting more open with my Michigan team, but I had to draw the line at telling them that I had a very lucrative job as a contractor with the government.

That was something nobody knew except Emma, and I preferred to keep it that way.

It wasn't that I didn't trust the people who were the most involved in Last Hope, but the less people who knew about my work the better it was for those top-secret projects.

In my mind, I'd already tasked the men who were most involved with Last Hope to keep enough secrets. They didn't need any more of that shit on their plates.

"I don't think that Emma and Wren really need a lot of financial support anymore," Brock said thoughtfully.

"They're going to get it anyway," I said hoarsely. "I fucking hate the fact that I have money and I wasn't there to help support Emma and my daughter when they really could have used that support."

"Emma's stubborn," Brock warned. "We wanted to help her with a few things years ago before her career really took off, and she flatly refused. She said she was perfectly capable of providing for her own daughter."

"I know that," I said unhappily. "She said I need to stop paying for things around the house and stop giving her things. But that's not going to happen. She's going to have to get used to me taking care of her and Wren."

"Maybe she's afraid you're doing it out of a sense of guilt," Brock suggested.

"I'm not," I said in a clipped voice. "Guilt isn't something I spend much time dwelling on. That shit will eat people alive. I'm doing it because I *want* to do it. I'm going to want to do the same for my daughter. That's not something I'm going to compromise on."

Hell, for the most part, I wasn't a guy who compromised…period. I was a man who gave orders and expected them to be carried out.

"You're going to have to be open to negotiation in the future," Brock informed me. "Emma isn't one of the men under your command. She'll be reasonable about letting you spend time with Wren, but you can't just tell her what to do."

I let out a frustrated breath. "I realize that. She's probably the most stubborn and the most infuriating woman on the planet sometimes."

Brock laughed. "That's probably why she intrigues you so much. She's incredibly kind, but she doesn't take orders well."

"I've noticed," I rumbled. "I suppose I'm going to have to learn to compromise…a little."

Brock smirked. "It's really not that painful if you care about someone. Maybe you should use a little of your own persistence and stubbornness to go after what you really want. I might be wrong, but I suspect that you've missed being with Emma since the day you parted. You just managed to put it out of your mind because being with her again was never a possibility."

I shook my head. "Even if that was what I wanted, I still don't have much to offer Emma. Last Hope has been my priority for a long time. I'm not going to change much at my age."

"I don't know," Brock mused. "You've seemed pretty damn content not thinking about Last Hope every minute of every day. It can still be a priority for you. It just doesn't have to consume your life all the time, Marshall. People can change at any age. We're actually sitting here having a personal discussion. That's never happened before."

"I've never had a personal life to talk about," I said gruffly.

"Probably because you've never wanted one before," Brock shot back. "Things have changed for you, Marshall. You'll have a daughter to think about in the future, and you could have Emma back in your life if that's what you really want."

I lifted a brow. "What makes you think that Emma would want a man like me in her life?"

Brock let out a disgusted sound. "I think the answer to that question is staring you in the face. Emma looks happier than I've ever seen her despite her kidnapping episode. Again, I could be wrong, but I think she's missed you since the day that you parted, too."

"The two of us are complete opposites, Brock," I argued.

He grinned. "I think you need her to shake up that orderly life of yours a little."

A little?

Emma had the ability to make me completely irrational.

That wasn't comfortable for a man like me.

The problem was, I wasn't certain that bothered me as much as I thought it would.

In some ways Emma's honesty and bluntness was starting to… amuse me.

Emma Lockwood's personality was growing on me, and I was finally able to admit that I'd miss everything about her when we were forced to separate again.

It wasn't *just* my dick that wanted her.

That chemistry had always been there between Emma and me.

The truth was, I wanted to be near Emma because I *liked* being close to her.

I was getting addicted to seeing her smile every day and her ability to just accept every fault that I had.

So much of our previous fling had been so focused on the outrageously good sex that I'd probably never noticed just how much I gravitated toward her just to be in the same room with her. That was a pretty startling admission for a guy who had spent almost every minute of the day alone for most of his life.

"Just think about it," Brock requested before he took another swig from his beer.

Oh, I'd think about it, whether I wanted to…or not.

I chugged the rest of my beer knowing that my thoughts had been consumed with Emma from the moment I'd found out that she was missing.

I doubted that was going to change anytime soon.

CHAPTER 17

Emma

"I like Colin," my best friend, Sara, informed me as I walked her to her car later that night. "He seems really interested in everything he can learn about Wren, and he's obviously been good to you since the kidnapping. You look at him like you're still crazy about him, Emma. What's the deal?"

The guys had already departed after watching the movie, and I'd walked Sara out so we could have a few moments to chat.

Sara was younger than me, but we'd been really close since she'd mysteriously moved to Cherry Cove years ago.

There wasn't much we didn't share, and I was pretty sure I knew most of her secrets that she didn't reveal to anyone else except me.

We'd talked and texted, but it was the first time I'd gotten to see her for any length of time since the kidnapping.

"He's been too good to me," I told her. "I can't seem to stop him from constantly buying me things. I can't mention wanting something without it magically appearing the next day. It's making me crazy."

"You're actually complaining about that?" she asked drily. "He's the man of most women's dreams if he's that attentive to your needs."

"I don't need him to buy me things," I said in a frustrated voice.

"What do you need from him? Obviously, you want him to be part of Wren's life, but I also think you're still crazy about him. I've known you for years, and I've never seen you look at another guy the way you look at him."

I nodded. Sara was the one person I talked to about everything. "Nothing has changed for me. He's just as gorgeous and irresistible as he was fourteen years ago. He thinks he's changed because of his injury to his leg, but he's still the same guy who made me do something completely out of character for me in Virginia Beach. There's something about Colin that makes every rational thought fly out of my head. It's stupid. It's been fourteen years."

"Maybe not so stupid," Sara said sympathetically as she leaned against her vehicle. "I'm not so sure you ever got over him. You've never been attracted to another guy. What if this is a second chance for you two? Maybe it's time for you to have that relationship you should have had years ago."

"That's not possible," I sputtered.

"Why not? You're both still single."

"It was a short fling fourteen years ago, Sara. Our lives are different. We aren't the same people we were then. He lives in San Diego. My life is in Cherry Cove. I'm almost forty-six with a teenage daughter. God, we never even discussed a relationship. We had sex. Lots and lots of amazing sex. And then we went our separate ways. That was the deal we made in Virginia Beach."

"You wanted more than that, Emma. I know you did. Apparently, Colin did, too. You said he went back to find you later that morning and you were already gone. Maybe you did have mind-blowing sex, but I think there was more than that for both of you. It just didn't happen that way because you both made that deal and you realized too late that you wanted more. It's not too late now."

I shook my head. "I don't think Colin is a relationship kind of guy."

I couldn't tell Sara about Last Hope or Colin's career, but I knew he was completely dedicated to both of them.

"You won't know that unless you ask him," she scolded. "The way he looks at you tells me he might be willing to try. Hell, have another fling with him if that's what it takes to make both of you see some sense. Dammit, Emma. You deserve to grab every bit of happiness you can get. You've dedicated your entire life to Wren and being a good mom. She's a teenager now. She doesn't need you to give up your life for her anymore, and she wouldn't want that. Wren is pretty independent and pretty mature for her age."

I snorted. "I might just offer him that fling until Wren gets home if I thought he'd take me up on it."

I was old enough to know that life was short and happiness could be fleeting.

It might kill me eventually when we had to say goodbye, but I wanted to be with Colin so much that I was almost willing to deal with the pain later to have an opportunity to be with him again.

Even if it was only for a little while.

"Seduce him," she said empathically. "Something tells me it wouldn't take much effort. Start there and see what happens. As your friend, I know I should be telling you to be cautious, but I also know you've carried a flame for this guy for years. Now that I've met him and spent some time watching you two, I think he feels the same way. Part of me wants you to be careful because you could end up with your heart broken. On the other hand, I don't want you to regret that you never even tried after the miracle of you two meeting up again. What were the chances of that?"

I knew she was right.

It *was* a miracle that we actually knew some of the same people and that our paths crossed one more time.

"I can't even explain what a shock it was for me to see him in Lania," I explained.

"He risked his life for you, Emma. And that was before he knew about Wren. God knows I'm not a woman who has any business giving relationship advice, but I think he might be a guy worth taking some risks for."

Sara didn't know about Last Hope, but she did know that Colin had been a SEAL commander. I'd told her that he'd volunteered to go to Lania to locate me because of his previous special forces experience.

She didn't know the details about how Brock and Nate had actually rescued me themselves.

All she knew was that they had gone to Lania to bring me home.

I hated deceiving my best friend, but I couldn't tell her the truth.

I completely understood the importance of keeping the existence of Last Hope a mystery to anyone who wasn't directly involved.

I had to let her continue to believe I'd been rescued by an active special forces team after Colin had located me.

Luckily, she'd been so relieved that I was safe that she hadn't asked for a bunch of details about the rescue. I'd given her the impression that I didn't want to talk about it and that I wanted to leave that experience behind me.

"I'm not saying he's not worth taking risks," I said hesitantly. "I'm just not sure he wants more than the fling we had years ago. I know he's still attracted to me, but that doesn't mean he wants to pick up where we left off."

"There's only one way to find out," she informed me.

Crap! I knew she was right, but putting myself out there was setting myself up for another heartbreak.

He's worth it, Emma. If he rejects you, at least you'll know that you tried.

I was getting to the point that possible heartbreak was less risky than living with the fact that I missed an opportunity that had been handed to me by a twist of fate.

I crossed my arms over my chest and looked at Sara. "Maybe I'll think about it after you admit that you have feelings for one of our male friends."

More than anything I really wanted my best friend to be happy. I was almost certain that she had a thing for one of the guys, but I'd never been able to get her to admit it.

It was possible that was something she hadn't even admitted to herself.

As expected, she simply rolled her eyes. "I don't. Every one of them is equally annoying and bossy, but I still consider them my friends, too. We were discussing Colin. Don't try to change the subject."

I let out a long sigh. "I don't know what to do. We're still attracted to each other, but everything has changed. We knew minimal information about our personal lives in Virginia Beach. Now, there isn't much we haven't shared. We're older now. Most of our fling centered around incredible sex. I'm not going to lie and say I don't still want that because Colin is seriously hot. Mostly, I just want to be with him in any way possible. I like seeing his handsome face in the morning and having it be the last thing I see every night. I really can't explain the way I feel. It's like something that's been missing from my life for a long time is just magically…there."

"He makes you happy," Sara said, summing up my feelings in four words.

"Yes," I admitted. "Even when we were having a fling he made me feel special. It never really felt like a fling. He listens to me like whatever I have to say is important. Yes, it drives me a little crazy because I can't mention I want something without him going out to get it for me the next day. But it's also pretty damn sweet. It's like he wants to make sure every want or need that I have is satisfied. He likes to act like a tough guy who doesn't have a heart, but I know better. Underneath all of that bluster and denial, Colin has the hugest heart I've ever seen. He just doesn't let people see it very often. And don't get me started on the way he still seems just as attracted to me as he was fourteen years ago. I have a mom body and I've aged a lot, but he still looks at me that same way that he did in Virginia Beach."

"Bodies change," Sara observed. "People change as they get older. You're still gorgeous, Emma, and that's all superficial. You're still the same woman you were years ago. If you're crazy about someone it doesn't really matter. I'm sure Colin has changed, but you accept him exactly the way he is now. Don't you think he had some insecurities about his limp and his injury? And he is older than you are."

I snorted. "He's still ridiculously fit and handsome. That imperfection just makes him a little more human. And we're only seven years apart in age. I'm going to be forty-six soon, and he just turned fifty-three a few months ago."

"I know you've been content to be Wren's mom and single," Sara said patiently. "But there's nothing wrong with wishing you had the *right* guy in your life."

Maybe I'd always buried that part of me that had been lonely all these years.

I'd put it aside because I knew that the man who had the ability to soothe that loneliness would never be in my life again.

"I didn't expect that guy to just pop up out of nowhere after all these years," I said drily.

"But he has," she reminded me. "And it's not like he's just going to disappear again. He's going to stay in your life because you share a daughter. It sounds like he really wants to be a dad to her in the future."

He did.

I already knew that.

Colin was eager to get to know his daughter.

He watched me do video calls with Wren every night, and I knew it killed him not to be part of those discussions.

He listened to her voice and her words like a man who was desperate to know his child.

"After he gets to know Wren, do you really want to just see him occasionally in passing when he visits with his daughter?" Sara asked.

"No," I confirmed in a tremulous voice. "I want so much more, but I'm not sure what I want is even possible."

My heart ached at the thought of only seeing Colin when he had a visit with Wren planned.

I wanted him to be part of my life, too. I just wasn't sure how to make that happen.

"For once in your life, do something crazy, Emma," Sara encouraged.

I had already done something crazy once in my life.

I'd had a fling fourteen years ago that had left my heart shattered.

I wasn't quite sure that I was brave enough to risk going through that all over again.

CHAPTER 18

Marshall

"Do you think they'll ever catch Nick's enemies?" Emma asked. "I'm worried that they haven't gotten the guys who were behind that whole assassination attempt and the kidnapping."

Even though it was late, neither one of us had been tired after Emma had finished her chat with Sara outside.

I'd grabbed Emma a glass of wine and another beer for myself before we'd headed out to the deck.

We were seated in the same loungers that Brock and I had occupied earlier.

"I'm working on it," I assured her. "These bastards are slippery and the kidnappers aren't talking, but I'll find them eventually."

Yeah, Nick was a friend and I cared about his safety, but my reason for tracking the kidnappers was intensely personal.

I wanted the assholes who had kidnapped Emma to get apprehended as quickly as possible.

"You're working on it yourself?" Emma asked curiously.

"Of course I'm working on it with Nick," I confirmed. "Do you really think I wouldn't be doing everything I can to catch the men who nearly killed you, Emma? Nick is throwing all of his resources toward it in Lania, but his governmental agencies just aren't as sophisticated as ours. Not to mention the fact that the US Government takes the kidnapping of US citizens pretty damn seriously."

"Do they know about the kidnapping?" she questioned.

I turned my head to look at her. With the porch light on I could see her puzzled expression.

"They know everything," I said jokingly. "You just won't always know what they know."

Tracking the men behind the kidnapping was a huge priority for our government right now, but I would have been doing the same thing I was already doing even if they weren't paying me to do it.

Lania had been a pain in the ass for the US for decades, and the last thing they wanted was more trouble and more kidnappings in the future.

"When I talked to Nick a few days ago, he didn't sound like he was worried about his own safety," Emma said unhappily.

"He's not," I admitted to her. "He's more worried about the fact that they kidnapped you and he's worried about the stability of his country. But he's not taking unnecessary risks, Emma. His bodyguards are surrounding him all the time. You don't need to keep fretting over his safety. They protected him from getting killed during the assassination attempt. The only one who suffered was you."

"I'm fine," she said dismissively. "He had his bodyguards. I had you and Last Hope to rescue me."

"Are you really fine, Emma?" I questioned with a frown.

She acted like she'd recovered well from her kidnapping, but I was still concerned.

Emma nodded earnestly. "I really am fine, Colin. I think the only thing that still bothers me is that awful assassination attempt. I'm afraid it will happen again and Nick won't be so lucky next time."

"Has it ever occurred to you that you could have been killed by one of those flying bullets?" I ground out.

She shook her head. "No. They weren't aiming at me. They wanted Nick."

Christ! Her nonchalant attitude drove me completely insane.

Bullets could ricochet and misplaced shots killed people all the time.

Thoughts of Emma being killed during that hail of bullets fucking haunted me all the damn time.

Hell, maybe it was better if she didn't know just how much danger she'd be in, but her offhandedness about her own safety irritated the hell out of me.

Just the thought of anything happening to her made my gut wrench.

"I'd prefer to never see you in that kind of situation again," I informed her.

That was putting it mildly.

I'd probably lose my shit if I had to go through that again.

Emma reached across the small table between us and put a hand on my forearm. "I'm safe, Colin. I don't think that's ever going to happen again."

The tension in my body relaxed...a little.

"I should hope not," I grumbled before I took a slug of my beer.

"You were really worried about me," she said softly after she'd swallowed a sip of her wine.

Worried?

Seeing Emma in danger terrified the hell out of me, and there were very few things that scared me after all of the years I'd spent working with the worst that humanity could offer.

"Of course I was worried," I answered, annoyed. "Why do you think I hauled my ass to Lania?"

She let out a long sigh. "Because you cared what happened to me even though we hadn't seen each other in years."

"It didn't matter how many years had passed," I muttered. "I think it's my job to worry about you. I don't think you do it often enough."

Emma always seemed concerned about everyone *except* herself.

Someone needed to pay attention to *her* needs, and I'd decided that person needed to be me.

Hell, maybe that was what happened when someone became an only parent to a child, but that shit had to stop.

Strangely, I'd started to enjoy being the one who looked after what Emma needed or wanted.

She laughed and the musical sound made my dick twitch.

"I'm a very mature adult, Colin," she reminded me teasingly.

"I don't give a shit," I rasped. "I want you to be happy and I want you to be safe."

"I want the same thing for you," she said as she stroked her fingertips up and down my forearm soothingly.

Something about the feeling of those soft fingers stroking my skin suddenly made me lose it.

I grabbed her wine and my beer, put them on the table, and shoved the table out of my way.

I yanked her lounger close to mine, wrapped my arms around her, and lifted her until she was sprawled across my body in my chair.

She gasped as she suddenly found herself on top of me.

I tightened my arms around her.

Yeah, that was *much* better.

I was convinced that there was no better feeling than having Emma as close to me as we could possibly get with our clothes on.

"Caveman," she accused without the least bit of annoyance as she snuggled into me.

I smirked as I stroked her silky hair. "That's not the first time you've called me that."

I had to admit that my feelings toward her had always been a little possessive and primal.

That hadn't changed for me.

And those instincts were almost impossible for me to ignore.

"I like your sometimes primitive behavior. I think I forgot that I thought it was really hot."

"It never scared you?" I asked, already knowing that Emma had never been afraid of me.

"Never," she said emphatically. "I always knew that beneath those Neanderthal instincts was a man who would rather hurt himself than hurt me. You were always protective of me and my feelings, Colin. I knew that."

Something broke inside of me when she put her head on my shoulder like she trusted me completely.

Hell, I'd rather cut my balls off with a dull knife than to betray that kind of trust in any way.

"I still feel that way, Emma," I confessed. "I think my first instinct is always going to be to protect you."

"I think that's just who you are," she said softly.

Not always.

But with her, it was *definitely* who I was.

I grunted as she wriggled on top of me to work her way up higher on my body.

The feel of that soft, curvy body moving over mine got my dick as hard as a pike in a nanosecond.

"Emma," I said in a warning voice, my heart pounding against my chest wall so violently that I had to take a deep breath to try to make it stop.

"What?" she said innocently as her beautiful, blue-eyed gaze met mine.

I threaded my hands into her hair. "I might be older, but I'm still a guy who finds this shapely body of yours incredibly appealing."

The need and affection in her eyes gutted me.

Fuck! This woman had always been my weakness, but I really didn't give a shit anymore.

I kissed her because I couldn't stop myself from doing it.

I ravaged her mouth like a desperate man, and when she returned the embrace with equal fervor, I knew I was fucked.

I finally allowed myself to touch Emma's gorgeous body as I kissed her, exploring every new curve and nuance that had gotten my dick hard the moment I'd seen her again.

I hadn't been trying to flatter her when I'd told her that I liked her curvier body.

Hell, I liked it far too much.

When I palmed the gorgeous ass I'd been admiring for days now, she moaned against my lips when I pulled her as tightly as I could against my aching cock.

Mine!

Emma Lockwood was fucking *mine*.

I wasn't a fanciful guy who believed in things like fate, but some primitive instinct told me that this woman was mine and was always meant to be mine.

I'd just been the idiot who had figured that out too damn late fourteen years ago.

Emma's eyes were glazed and she was breathless when I reluctantly released her mouth.

I wasn't going to lie.

There was a masculine part of me that was damn satisfied that she was just as affected by me as I was by her.

"Colin," she said in a needy tone that made me want to carry her to bed and satisfy every damn need she had.

She hugged me so tightly around the neck that I could barely breathe, but I savored every second of it.

I decided that breathing was highly overrated.

I didn't really need to breathe right now.

I needed *her*.

Probably always had.

Definitely always would.

I was too damn old to lie to myself.

"I think we should have another fling," she finally said as she clung to me. "We have time before Wren comes home. I just want to spend that time being with you. I know it sounds crazy. I'm not asking for commitments or a future. I just want to live in the moment this one time and be with you."

My baser instincts were telling me to take her up on that offer before she could change her mind.

However…

"Not happening," I said flatly.

Her body tensed, so I went on to explain. "I want to be with you, Emma, but it isn't going to be a fling. You mean more to me than a fuck or two. I'm not going to pretend that you don't. I'm too old and set in my ways for bullshit. I'm down for living in the moment, but we're going to actually date. It's what I actually wanted years ago, but I was too afraid to admit it. We had a deal and I stuck to it. No deals this time. We'll figure out the future later, but I'm going to treat you the way you deserve to be treated *before* we have sex. We did things ass backwards last time. That isn't happening again."

She groaned as she released her tight grip on my neck. "It's not going to be easy for me to keep my hands off you."

I grinned. "I never said that you had to keep your hands off me. Honestly, I prefer that you don't because I already know that I'll definitely be touching you. I'm just saying that we're not having sex until you know that there's more between us than just the physical. Hell, it won't be easy for me, either, but I want a hell of a lot more than we had years ago. Figure out where you want to go on our first date tomorrow, and we'll start living in the moment together. I'm probably going to suck at it because my instinct is to plan everything carefully."

"How do you feel about going to Mackinac Island?" she asked.

"I've heard about it, but I've never been there," I admitted.

I knew that it was an island that prohibited motor vehicles, so it wasn't possible to drive around there, but the photos I'd seen of the island had been picturesque.

"I haven't been for a long time," Emma said wistfully. "But I love it there."

"I'll book a hotel. Pack a bag in the morning. We'll stay for a few days."

Hell, if Emma was longing to go there, I'd stay there as long as she wanted.

I didn't really care where we went as long as she was with me.

I could deal with living in the moment with Emma if that's what she was comfortable with right now.

At some point in the future, we were going to be done with living in the moment and the end result would be exactly what I really wanted.

Yeah, I still had some reservations about whether or not I'd make a good partner to her, but…bottom line…there wasn't another guy in the world that would work as hard as I would to make sure that she was happy.

I'd fucking learn to compromise.

I'd learn to be emotionally available for her.

I'd learn to be the man that she needed.

I'd learn to deal with the fact that she was the only person in the world who could make me completely irrational.

Emma Lockwood *would* be mine.

I had no choice but to make that happen in the future.

I was a smart guy, and I wasn't about to blow a second chance at getting exactly what I'd wanted since those days we'd spent together in Virginia Beach.

I'd been an idiot back then, but I wasn't about to make the same monumental mistake twice in one lifetime.

The only thing that would stop all that from happening was if Emma didn't feel the same way.

That part of the equation was out of my control, but I'd do everything possible to increase my chances of getting what I wanted.

I'd just have to hope that was going to be enough.

CHAPTER 19

Emma

Living in the moment with Colin turned out to be far easier than I'd originally thought it would be.

We'd taken the ferry to Mackinac Island late yesterday morning. He'd patiently let me drag him around the island to see the sights.

Honestly, everything we'd done together had felt as natural as breathing for me.

Colin had seemed to like every activity. He'd actually seemed to enjoy the butterfly conservatory, and he'd been the one to arrange a horse-drawn carriage tour himself.

The carriage tour was a little cheesy and touristy, but I'd loved every romantic second of it with Colin.

We were staying for three nights. I'd protested when he'd booked a lake view room at the Grand Hotel because it was ridiculously pricy, but he'd blown off the expense like it was nothing.

After we'd arrived, he claimed that it was worth every penny when we'd taken in the views from the world's longest porch at the Victorian-era hotel.

The Grand Hotel was iconic, and I'd always wanted to stay there, but it was way too pricy when there were options that were way cheaper and nice on the island.

"Are you getting tired?" Colin asked as we brought our bikes to a stop when we reached Arch Rock. "It's getting hot."

We'd rented bikes to do the circuit around the island.

I swiped my hand over my sweaty forehead, surprised when I saw that the ride hadn't even worked up a sweat on Colin.

Nor was he even slightly out of breath.

In fact, he looked impossibly handsome and perfectly comfortable in his jeans and a lightweight T-shirt.

I was perspiring in a pair of capri pants and a lightweight tee.

The ride around the island wasn't terribly long. It was a little over eight miles, and we were stopping often. But it had been a long time since I'd spent any significant time on a bicycle.

I was hot and it was humid beneath the summer sun, and I was definitely getting my cardio today.

"I'm hot," I admitted as we pushed our bikes to a safe area. "I'm looking forward to hitting that beautiful pool at the hotel later."

Colin stowed our bikes and immediately handed me my water bottle. "We'll rest for a while here. You need more sunscreen before we head back."

I smiled at him before I took the hand he offered me. "I think I'm getting old. This bike ride was a lot easier when I was a kid."

Colin shot me a huge grin that made my heart melt. "I think we were just oblivious to the heat and humidity when we were younger," he answered.

We were both wearing sunglasses, but that smile took my breath away even though I couldn't see his eyes.

My heart squeezed inside my chest.

The man who never smiled was becoming a man who had no problem enjoying life.

Little by little, Colin was…changing.

The coolness and the distance I'd felt with him in the very beginning was starting to completely disappear when we were together.

I couldn't say that he was the same man that he'd been in Virginia Beach. It was hard to compare since we'd known almost nothing personal about each other then.

Honestly, it was better than it had ever been in Virginia Beach. This relationship felt a lot more…real.

Right now, he seemed incredibly…happy.

I knew that same happiness was radiating from me even though I was hot, tired, and sweaty.

Colin had switched into *dating* mode with me effortlessly.

He was attentive.

Affectionate.

And he was open in a way I'd never seen him in the past.

He either took my hand or wrapped an arm around me possessively whenever we were together.

It was almost like the change between us was instinctual and natural for him.

And his actions meant everything to me.

Colin had always treated me like I was special, but now I felt like the only woman in the world who existed as far as he was concerned.

He might not be a conventionally charming guy, but his genuine concern and affection were way more endearing than all of the bullshit charm in the world.

Granted, he'd bought me far too much Mackinac Island fudge, but he'd helped me devour it when I'd declared that I couldn't eat another bite.

The man spoiled me shamelessly, and for a woman who had never had that in her life, it was an almost overwhelming but achingly sweet experience.

Yeah, he went overboard sometimes, but I was starting to realize that it was his way of letting me know that he cared because he wasn't always good with words.

Colin suddenly stopped, released my hand, took my water bottle from me and opened it. "Drink," he demanded. "You'll end up dehydrated in this kind of heat if you don't."

"Bossy," I teased but took the bottle gratefully.

"Concerned," he corrected.

I drank until my thirst was satisfied and handed the bottle to Colin.

He shook his head.

"Drink it," I insisted. "I'm done for now and we have another bottle on the bikes."

He had to be thirsty, but he acted like he didn't want to take any water away from me in case I needed it.

It was incredibly sweet, but totally unnecessary.

As expected, he slammed the rest of the water down the moment I'd assured him that I was done with it.

He had been sacrificing…for me.

No wonder I was crazy about this man.

He always put my needs first.

He'd always been that way, even in Virginia Beach.

His behavior had been almost unimaginable for me after being married to a man who had dumped me because I supposedly couldn't have a child.

My ex had also been incredibly selfish and mean in other ways, too.

It wasn't until I met Colin that I realized how much I'd been missing in a romantic relationship.

Maybe Colin and I hadn't really had a relationship, but he'd taught me a lot about the way I wanted to be treated.

He'd essentially spoiled me for any other man.

Colin had come into my life at a time when I wasn't feeling good about myself.

I'd been completely crushed emotionally and physically.

During our time in Virginia Beach, I realized that I *was* valuable.

That my opinions *did* matter.

That I deserved to be respected.

That I was still desirable.

And I'd refused to settle for anything less in the future.

I'd never found anyone like Colin again, but I was glad I'd never settled.

If I had, I wouldn't be with the man I was crazy about right at this very moment.

"Are you okay, Em?" Colin questioned in a concerned voice as he took my hand again.

God, I loved it when he called me by that old, shortened pet name he'd occasionally used in Virginia Beach.

From him, it sounded like an endearment.

"Yeah," I assured him as I pulled myself out of my thoughts. "I was just thinking about what an amazing guy you are."

He frowned at me. "I think that then I'm going to start to wonder about your mental competence. I'm a complete asshole, Emma. Ask anyone who knows me."

"Then they don't really know you," I argued as we positioned ourselves to get a nice view of the limestone arch and the stunning views of Lake Michigan. "I think you're the most incredible man I've ever known."

He shrugged. "Since I like the fact that you think that, I guess I'll let you stay delusional."

I slapped him on the shoulder playfully. "Stop that! You *are* amazing. You just don't realize it."

Colin might not see all of the qualities that I adored about him, but they were definitely there.

He might do a good job of hiding them from the rest of the world, but I'd always been able to see right through his tough guy act.

He grinned at me as he pulled his phone out of his pocket. "Keep those delusions coming, sweetheart. Picture."

I shook my head. "No photos. I look sweaty and disgusting right now."

"You look stunningly gorgeous," he replied as he wrapped his arm around me, positioned the two of us, and held the phone out as far as possible to get the picturesque scenery behind us.

"Okay, which one of us is delusional now?" I said jokingly.

"Not me," he insisted. "Smile."

Crap! Any makeup I'd put on earlier was long gone, but if he still thought I looked gorgeous, I could hardly refuse.

The truth was, I'd have him AirDrop that photo to me later because I wanted every picture of the two us here that I could get.

We weren't talking about the future, and I wanted to conserve every single memory of our time together.

I smiled and he clicked the photo.

"Happy now?" I teased as he shoved the phone back into his pocket.

He wrapped his arms around my waist and pulled me against his massive body. "I am now," he said huskily as he tightened his arms around me.

I put my arms around his neck, both of us completely ignoring the other people who were enjoying the views with us.

"I probably stink," I warned him. "I'm still sweaty."

He leaned down until his lips were close to my ear. "As I recall, we both liked to be hot and sweaty together. Neither one of us ever complained."

I suddenly felt a whole lot hotter than I had moments ago.

"I thought we weren't thinking about that right now," I said breathlessly.

His lips still near my ear, he said huskily, "Oh, I think about it, Em. I fucking think about it every damn time I see you."

A shiver of heat ran down my body and straight between my thighs.

My body craved this man, and it was getting harder and harder to keep those desires in check for me.

I wanted to be as close to Colin as I could get, and my body ached with the need to be that intimately connected as soon as possible.

"Colin," I said in a needy voice as I stared up at him.

"Kiss me, Em," he urged hoarsely. "For now, just fucking kiss me."

I pulled his head down, and Colin did the rest.

The kiss probably looked a little desperate to the tourists around us, but neither one of us really noticed.

We were just two people who momentarily got lost in each other.

I savored that embrace for as long as I possibly could.

I could feel how much he wanted me and cared about me without the two of us exchanging a single word.

For now, that was more than enough.

CHAPTER 20

Marshall

"What are you going to tell Wren about Last Hope and your job?" Emma asked as we got ready to go to bed that night.

We'd taken advantage of the pool at the hotel earlier.

Strangely, I wasn't nearly as self-conscious about the scars on my leg.

I wasn't going to say that I'd forgotten that I had them, but if Emma accepted them just fine, I didn't really care what anybody else thought anymore.

She'd wanted me to swim with her, and I wanted to make her happy.

Seeing that smile on her face when I'd agreed to go into the pool with her made the awkwardness of baring my injured leg disappear for me.

Truthfully, nobody stared at my leg like it was horrible.

People were so involved in their own lives and their own vacations that they didn't seem to notice.

We'd had a good dinner and gone for a walk after we'd eaten.

Normally, I was a guy who was always busy doing something productive from the time I got up to the time I turned in at night.

It wasn't like that when I was with Emma.

Everything we did together, no matter how insignificant, seemed... important.

"As little as possible," I said as I got into bed beside her. I'd thought about booking two rooms, but we were used to sleeping together, and she'd nixed that idea the moment I'd mentioned it. I'd been relieved because I wasn't sure I would have slept worth a damn without her with me. "Probably as much as you told her about your kidnapping."

Emma had chosen not to discuss her kidnapping with her mother and Wren so they could enjoy their time together.

She'd simply told them that she'd been in an area without cell coverage for a while.

She sighed. "I'll have to tell them the truth eventually. I don't lie to either of them. My daughter is going to ask more questions about my trip to Lania when she gets home. She's excited about being in California right now, but she'll ask all about the trip. I've always been as honest as possible with Wren."

Emma snuggled closer to me, and I automatically wrapped an arm around her to pull her as close to my body as she could get.

It was an instinctive reaction that was becoming normal for me.

For a guy who had been single his entire life, that was probably odd behavior.

Hell, I didn't know what was normal or abnormal for me anymore.

My entire world had been upended from the moment I'd seen Emma's picture on Wyatt's phone.

I was resigned to the fact that I was never going to be the same man I was before that happened.

Honestly, I didn't really *want* to be that solitary, miserable bastard anymore.

"I'm not planning on lying to her," I informed Emma. "I'd just like to delay telling her as long as possible. Most of what I do is pretty dark. It's not something a kid needs to think about."

"She's not a young child anymore, Colin," she explained. "Even though she's my only child, I've tried not to be a helicopter parent. I know I can't shield her from everything unpleasant that happens in the world. That's not going to prepare her for adulthood someday. I did hold off on getting her a cell phone until her thirteenth birthday, and I watch her screen time so it doesn't rot her adolescent brain. But she's smart and she asks a lot of questions about things that are happening in the world. I answer her as honestly as possible. It's a delicate balance sometimes. You want your kid to be a kid, but you don't want them to be so naïve that someone can take advantage of that. Having a gifted daughter isn't always easy. I don't want to let her skip another grade. I know she'll be starting college a little earlier than most kids already. She just turned thirteen."

I already knew my daughter's birthday.

I couldn't fault Emma for not wanting Wren to skip another grade.

If she did, Wren wouldn't be much over sixteen when she started college.

Although her intelligent brain might be ready for college, it was a lot to handle emotionally for a girl that age.

Emma was already looking into letting Wren take some college courses while she was still in high school to keep my daughter from getting bored.

I knew that would have helped me if I'd had that option when I was young.

"You're doing everything right," I assured her.

I could tell from listening to their conversations that Emma and Wren had built a relationship that was made of trust and love.

"I'm going to fuck up," I added, telling Emma one of my greatest fears.

Emma chuckled. "All parents screw up," she shared. "All we can do is love our kids and hope we don't screw them up too much. I've made more than my fair share of mistakes, Colin, and Wren has turned out to be a good kid anyway."

"You've done all the hard work," I grumbled. "I don't want to enter her life and mess all of that up at this point. I know nothing about kids."

I'd had my moments when I'd wondered if Wren would be better off without an inept father.

I wasn't about to forget that she existed and just walk away. I wanted to be part of my daughter's life. I just wasn't sure how to be a father.

Emma sighed as she stroked a hand over my bare chest. "I know this has to be hard for you. It's something you didn't expect. Wren has been part of my life for almost fourteen years."

"Having a kid was never even on my radar," I admitted.

What in the hell did I know about young girls and what they needed from a parent?

I spent most of my waking moments talking to and interacting with men who had been in the special forces at one time.

"She's getting to the age where all she needs is guidance," Emma explained. "I'm kind of relieved that you'll be around for her high school years. I've tried my best to understand my intellectually gifted daughter, but I didn't experience that myself. You did. I think there's some things that you can guide her on that I can't."

"Don't sell yourself short, Em," I said in a graveled voice. "Wren grew up with a parent who loved and accepted her. That's the important part. I grew up as a confused foster kid who never felt normal. I didn't really find my family until I got into the Naval Academy. Having my life more structured and being around other intelligent young adults helped me a lot."

"What happened to your parents?" she asked softly.

Hell, that part of my life had happened so long ago that I didn't really think about it anymore. "They died when I was six, so I barely remember either one of them now. They were heavily involved in volunteer work. They slowed down on traveling around the world helping the less fortunate when I was born, but they decided to take one last international trip. I stayed with one of their friends. The two of them were kidnapped, tortured, and killed. Neither of them had close family who wanted to take me on, so I ended up in foster care."

"That must have been so traumatic for you," she said in a troubled voice. "Is that why you do what you do now?"

"Maybe," I said offhandedly. "I've never really thought about it, but I guess I never wanted to see another kid lose their parents because no one was there to get them out before it was too late."

"You were only six," she said softly. "I'm surprised you weren't adopted."

"I'm not," I said drily. "I was a weird kid, even at the age of six. I didn't socialize well with kids my age. I preferred to read and learn rather than play with other kids my age. I didn't fit in. That's why I told you not to sell yourself short. Having a parent who makes you feel normal is everything to a child. You've been an incredible mom to Wren."

"I think she still feels different sometimes," Emma answered. "But she's starting to accept that being unique is okay."

"She'll accept it more as she gets older," I told her. "It's hard not fitting in with other kids when you're young."

"She's incredibly gifted with computers and technology," Emma said. "I wish I knew more, but her skills are getting way above my head. I know enough to do my job and normal things, but I'm not a whiz with software and the intricate details of programming."

"Okay," I said grudgingly. "Maybe I can be somewhat useful in that area."

"You can be useful in a lot of ways," Emma scolded. "Just love her, Colin. She's never said anything to me, but I think she's always wanted to know her father. It just wasn't possible before for her."

"What if she resents the fact that I haven't been around for her?" I asked cautiously. "I have a lot of regrets about missing her childhood."

"Don't," Emma said firmly. "We can't change the past, Colin. Wren knows that it wasn't your fault that you didn't know about her. You're here for her now. I know my daughter. She's not going to be resentful. I think she's going to be happy."

Hell, I hoped that was true.

I knew she was right.

Regrets weren't going to get me anywhere, and they weren't going to help me be a good parent to my daughter now.

I was going to have to accept the fact that I hadn't been there for Emma or my daughter during Wren's childhood and move on.

"Life is going to be different for you and Wren from now on," I warned her. "I *will* be paying for expenses and whatever college education she wants."

"I have a college fund for her," Emma argued. "I'm saving a lot more now that my income is higher."

"I want the account number," I insisted. "I'll make damn sure you never have to contribute another penny."

"Just like that?" she teased.

I nodded. "Just like that. I told you that I'm not hurting for money, Em. I have no debt and more money than I know what to do with most of the time. Even my home in San Diego is paid off. You don't have to struggle to raise our daughter alone anymore."

"Things have gotten a lot easier," she said. "I make a lot more money than I did when Wren was younger. I wish I could say that my home is completely paid for, but we do just fine. I don't want your money, Colin. I just want you to be in Wren's life."

"I am going to be in her life, but paying the future expenses is not negotiable," I informed her. "I've missed thirteen years of paying child support and expenses."

"Maybe," she teased. "But the really expensive years are coming up."

"I'll handle those," I said in a no-nonsense tone. "I plan on being in Wren's life. I'm hoping that you'll let me be part of your life, too, Emma."

Her body stiffened a little before she said lightly, "I thought we were just living in the moment."

"Is that what you want?" I asked gruffly.

Hell, I was trying to live in the moment, but I was quickly realizing that I sucked at doing that.

I was a guy who planned everything.

I wanted to know that Emma was going to be in my life after Wren came home and beyond.

After being with Emma again, I couldn't imagine a future without her in my life.

I wanted to be there as a goddamn partner to her, like I should have been from the very beginning.

"I just know that I want to be with you," she murmured as she ran an exploring hand over my body. "It still seems surreal that you're actually here."

I wrapped my fingers around her wrist to stop her exploring fingers from moving over my skin.

Fucking hell! This woman was going to be the death of me one day.

I was fifty-three years old.

I wasn't the younger, hornier guy I'd been when we'd first met.

However, my need to claim Emma as mine was so sharp that it was almost physically painful.

I'd waited almost fourteen fucking years to do just that, and my patience was running pretty thin.

Being with Emma like this was almost torturous.

"I'm sorry," she said breathlessly. "I know we're older, but I still want to get you naked."

Hell, I wanted the same thing.

My desire for Emma was still just as strong as it had been years ago, but it was also somewhat…different.

I rolled on top of her and pinned her hands over her head. "Do you really think I don't want the same thing?" I rasped as I looked down at her beautiful face.

I wanted to make love to Emma and worship her body like I should have done years ago.

I was consumed by a possessiveness and a need to make Emma mine that I'd managed to ignore all those years ago.

That shit wasn't happening again.

I was too old for that.

I *knew* what I wanted because I'd been without Emma for way too long.

I'd missed this woman since the day we'd parted. I'd just never admitted it to myself or anyone else because it would have been pointless.

She shook her wrists loose and wrapped her arms around my neck. "Then just make love to me, Colin," she said insistently. "Let's not think about the future right now. Just be with me."

My dick ached and my gut twisted at the need I could see in her gorgeous eyes as I scanned her face.

I closed my eyes.

Miraculously, Emma *still* wanted me.

I could see it.

I could *feel* it.

I could hear the need in her voice.

For *me*.

She hadn't been with or wanted another man since the two of us had been together in Virginia Beach.

I fought for the control that should be easier at my age, but I knew that knowledge was about to break me in a way that nothing ever had before.

CHAPTER 21

Emma

I could tell that Colin was fighting with himself.

That was the last thing I wanted.

I was a mature adult, and I knew exactly what I wanted.

Maybe he was afraid to make promises that he couldn't keep in the future, so I wanted to reassure him that I wasn't asking him for anything he didn't want to give.

"I just want to be with you, Colin," I assured him. "I'm not asking for a future."

There was never going to be another man for me.

Colin had always been the man for me, and I was tired of making excuses for not reaching out and taking what I wanted. Even if it was only for a little while.

He opened his eyes and skewered me with the intensity in his stormy gaze.

"What if I want there to be a future for us?" he asked in a rough tone.

He'd phrased it as a question, so I was assuming that he wasn't quite sure what he wanted, but that it could be a future together.

My heart skipped a beat, but I didn't flinch as I stared right back at him.

God, I wanted that.

I *wanted* a future with Colin so much that my heart ached with that longing.

"If this is going to happen, don't ask me to just walk away," he said hoarsely. "I don't think I'm capable of doing that again, Em."

The vulnerability in his voice made my heart squeeze so tightly it was painful.

Colin was a man who never let anyone see his vulnerabilities, but I knew they existed.

Most people probably thought he was an impenetrable, emotionless fortress that could never be breached.

I knew that wasn't true.

His emotions ran deep. He was just better at hiding them than everyone else.

I stroked the back of his neck. "I'll never ask you to do that," I reassured him.

I'd never wanted him to do that the first time, but I'd been too damn afraid of breaking the agreement we'd made to ask for something more.

Some weird twist of fate had thrown the two of us together again, and I wasn't about to toss this opportunity aside.

I didn't know what our future looked like, but I knew that I'd missed Colin so much that I ached for him.

I needed to be as close to him as I could possibly get.

Yes, that need was sexual, but it was also highly emotional for me now.

"Good," he said in a husky, relieved tone. "Because I'm about to explore the sexy, curvy body you complain about all the time."

Heat pooled between my thighs and I let out a needy sigh as he stroked a hand down my body until he got to the hem of the nightgown that was tangled around my thighs.

Colin shifted so he could pull the nightgown up to my waist and over my head.

I sat up, trying not to think about how much my body had changed over the years.

I shivered as his fingers skimmed over my bare skin.

I was self-conscious about my curvy body and the faded stretch marks on my belly, but it had been so long since Colin had touched me like this that part of me really didn't care.

"Could you turn the light off?" I asked hesitantly.

"No," he said flatly. "You're still the most beautiful woman I've ever seen. I want to be able to see you."

I laid my head back on the pillow with a snort as his hands started to explore my body. "Which part do you find attractive?" I asked jokingly. "My plumpness or the stretch marks on my belly?"

He traced a finger over the faded marks on my abdomen. "You carried my child, Emma," he said huskily like that fact was a miracle to him. "If you think that's not sexy, you're wrong. And I happen to like your curvy body."

"You're insane," I accused. "Nobody thinks that stretch marks are hot."

"I do," he said earnestly as his body covered mine. "There's not a damn thing about you that isn't sexy."

I wrapped my arms around his neck as my body relaxed and melted against his harder form.

He wasn't lying.

I could feel his hard cock pressing against me, and every negative thought I'd had about my changed body slipped out of my brain.

I suddenly realized that my insecurities about my body were old baggage. My ex had hated it when I was curvier, and he'd always told me that it was a complete turnoff.

Somehow, that trash had burrowed its way into my brain so deeply that it was in my subconscious, and it was time for that to go.

I thought I'd expelled every negative thought from my head regarding my ex a long time ago, but there was obviously one more that needed to get tossed out of my psyche.

Colin wasn't my ex, and he obviously did like my curvy body, stretch marks included.

"Colin," I said in a needy whisper as I closed my eyes. "I need…"

My desire for this man was endless and my entire body was aching with the desperation to feel him inside of me.

"I'll take care of all of your needs," he told me as his mouth skimmed my jawline. "But I'm not rushing this, Emma."

I moaned against his lips as his mouth came down hard to claim mine.

Desire consumed me as Colin devoured my mouth like a man who had been deprived of sustenance for eons.

I kissed him back with the same desperation, relishing the hunger in his embrace.

It had been so long since I'd felt this kind of raw emotion, and I reveled in it because I knew it was only possible with *this* man.

I ran my hands over his back as he released my mouth, needing to feel every inch of his powerful body.

"Touch me, Em," he encouraged as he explored the sensitive skin of my neck with his lips.

"I love your body," I said as I touched every inch of bare skin I could find with my fingertips.

"Not nearly as much as I love yours," he said in a deep baritone as he worked his way down my body to my breasts.

My back arched up as he covered one of my nipples with his hot mouth and tormented it with his tongue and teeth.

My core clenched so hard from the erotic sensation that a whimper escaped my lips.

"Colin," I murmured as I threaded my fingers into his short hair.

"You make me fucking crazy, Emma," he growled as he moved to torture my other breast. "I'm not sure I like feeling this way at my age."

"I like it," I said as I panted from the ecstasy that was consuming my body.

I loved the fact that I could make Colin as crazy as he made me feel.

"You're so damn beautiful, Em," he grunted as his lips touched the marks on my belly in a worshipful way that brought tears to my eyes.

I *felt* beautiful for the first time in fourteen years.

I *felt* desirable.

I *felt* wanted.

No other man had ever made me feel this way, and I'd thought I'd never feel that way again.

My emotions were all over the place as Colin skimmed my panties down my legs and tossed them on the floor.

But the moment he parted my thighs and his fingers stroked over my wet pussy, all I could do was feel what he was doing to my body.

I lifted my hips with a moan, trying to get exactly what my body needed.

I craved Colin's touch, and I needed…more.

"Oh, God," I said in a mesmerized voice that I hardly recognized as my own.

I knew Colin intimately, and I knew what was coming.

He was a guy who had absolutely no issues with giving a woman oral sex as long and as often as possible.

In fact, it was something he seemed to enjoy, which just made it even hotter.

I felt like a huge bolt of electricity shot down my spine when his mouth came down on me and his tongue stroked over my clit.

A helpless moan escaped from my lips as Colin gripped my ass and devoured me in a carnal way that made me completely insane.

He knew exactly how to pleasure my body, and the intimacy of the way that he did it was sublime.

"Colin!" I whimpered, gripping his short locks until it was probably painful for him.

He didn't complain.

He groaned against my pussy, and I felt those vibrations so acutely that the knot in my belly started to slowly unfurl.

Colin expertly increased the pressure on my clit, and explored my wet channel with one finger, and then two.

He fucked me with those fingers, and I knew that I was going to climax.

My body couldn't take this kind of intense pleasure without imploding.

It had been so long for me, and the sensations were overwhelming.

"Please," I begged. "Make me come."

I wasn't sure I could take much more without completely losing my mind.

When those wicked fingers inside me curled and found my G-spot, it was over for me.

I screamed Colin's name over and over again as my core clenched tightly around his fingers.

My body shook with the force of my climax, and I was gasping for breath by the time it finally ended.

Dear God! I hadn't realized I was still capable of having an orgasm like this one.

It was so sharp and so forceful that it was almost frightening.

I trembled in the aftermath, and Colin slid up my body and wrapped his arms around me tightly.

"Christ, Em!" he said hoarsely before he kissed me and then buried his face in my hair. "You're the most responsive woman I've ever known."

"Only because you're the hottest guy on the planet," I panted, my body still trying to recover. "Fuck me, Colin. I need you."

My body was somewhat satiated, but that didn't calm the aching need to have him inside me.

I'd craved that feeling, and that hadn't gone away.

He knew I was on birth control for my PCOS, and that a pregnancy with my condition was highly improbable anyway, so we didn't need to have that discussion.

Neither one of us had been with anyone else, so we didn't need to have the condom discussion, either.

"No fucking this time," he growled as he took off his boxer briefs. "I'm going to make love to you. And it's going to mean something to me. You'll be mine after this, Em. I hope you're ready for that."

I shivered in anticipation at the possessiveness in his voice.

This big, burly, beautiful man wanted to claim *my* body.

There was nothing hotter than that because I desperately *wanted* to be claimed.

I wrapped my arms around his neck. "I'm beyond ready. It's been a long time for us."

"Too damn long," he rasped as his body covered mine.

One powerful thrust and he was exactly where I needed him.

I gasped out loud as time stopped for me while I savored the raw intimacy of having him buried deep inside me.

"You feel so good," I moaned.

"I've wanted this from the moment I saw you again, Emma," he said hoarsely, his warm breath wafting across my ear.

My heart swelled inside my chest until it felt like it was going to explode.

I'd wanted him, too.

So badly that it hurt.

I wrapped my legs around his waist and met every thrust of his cock.

We got completely lost in each other's bodies.

Every touch.

Every surge of his cock thrusting inside me.

Every feel of his lips on my skin.

The sexuality and carnality were still there, but there was so much...more.

I felt like Colin was claiming me with every action, and I loved feeling like I was actually his.

It was hot.

It was so intimate that tears filled my eyes.

He started slow, but things got out of control quickly.

"Colin," I moaned as he pummeled in and out of my body.

I suddenly realized that I loved this man so fiercely that it took my breath away.

I love him.

I probably always had and always would.

Maybe I'd been an idiot not to realize it before because it felt like those emotions had always been there.

I'd just never wanted to admit that I loved a man who was supposed to be a fling.

"Emma," he groaned before his lips came down on mine.

I felt taken.

I felt consumed by this man.

That probably should have scared the hell out of me, but it didn't.

I was too lost in the sensations of being this intimately connected to Colin.

My head thrashed on the pillow when he released my mouth.

"I want…" I said tremulously. "I need…"

"I know, sweetheart," he said roughly as his hand slipped between our bodies and stroked my clit. "Come for me. I want to watch you get off."

And my body imploded.

I went up in flames as Colin pounded into me like a madman.

I screamed his name as my core clenched tightly around his cock.

"So damn beautiful," he groaned as I climaxed and milked him to his own release.

My entire body was shaking as he rolled and pulled me on top of his massive body.

Neither one of us spoke as we recovered our breath and our heartbeats started to slow to a normal rhythm again.

I had a moment of vulnerability because I'd finally admitted to myself that I loved Colin.

Maybe he sensed that vulnerability because his arms tightened around me until I felt protected.

I'd just have to hope he'd protect my heart in the future, too.

CHAPTER 22

Marshall

Holy fucking hell!
This woman was definitely going to be the death of me, but at least I'd die the happiest idiot in existence because I was with *her*.

I held Emma tightly as my heart rate slowed back to normal.

We might be older, but the chemistry between the two of us hadn't changed.

As far as I was concerned, she'd just sealed her fate by letting me touch her and get inside her beautiful body.

She *was* mine.

She wanted me.

I wanted her.

It was a done deal.

Okay, she hadn't exactly made me promises for a future, but she'd agreed to never make me walk away from her again.

I knew I wasn't fucking going anywhere, so I'd find a way to make damn sure that we had a future.

"We're sweaty and I feel like a total mess," Emma murmured against my shoulder.

"Don't move," I demanded. "I like it when you're a sweaty mess."

I'd forgotten exactly what it felt like to be with Emma this way, and I wanted to stretch this moment out a little longer.

My dick was finally content, and I was actually...happy.

Hell, I'd forgotten what happiness felt like, and I wanted to reacquaint myself with that particular emotion as often as possible.

I'd been a restless, discontented asshole for almost fourteen years.

I didn't have that many days left when I'd be sleeping in the same bed with Emma, and I wasn't going to take those nights for granted.

I'd rented a vacation place down the street from Emma, and I'd be moving to that location before Wren got home from San Diego.

While Emma had insisted that I could stay with her, I knew it wasn't going to make a good first impression on my daughter if I was sleeping with her mother.

I wanted to get to know my daughter, but she didn't need me in her face every moment of the day.

She'd need some space, and I was going to give her what she needed.

I planned on staying in Cherry Cove for a few weeks until it was time for Wren to start high school.

Emma and I hadn't really discussed what would happen when the summer was over, but I'd figure it out after I'd gotten to know my daughter.

"What are you thinking about?" Emma asked as she lifted her head to look at me.

"You and Wren," I readily admitted truthfully.

"You're nervous about meeting her," Emma stated.

Hell yes, I was nervous, and I didn't like it.

I was a guy who could handle stressful situations and always had all of the answers.

For the first time in my life I had no idea how to handle a situation.

I couldn't control how she'd feel.

I couldn't control whether or not she actually wanted her father to stroll into her life at the age of thirteen.

I didn't like not having complete control over every detail of my life.

"In general, I'm not really a likeable guy, Emma."

"That's not true," she protested. "I like you."

"Yeah," I grumbled as my arm tightened around her waist. "I never really did understand that."

"Once you let your guard down and allow someone to really know you, it's impossible not to like you," she insisted.

Well, that was a little problematic since I almost never let my guard down.

"Social relationships have never been easy for me," I admitted grudgingly. "Give me a problem to solve, and I can do it. Put me in a social situation and I suck at it."

"That's because your intelligent brain is always working to solve problems," Emma said softly as she ran a soothing hand over my chest. "Wren has the same struggles sometimes, but she's adjusting. She's not going to need you to solve her problems, Colin. She's a smart girl and getting more independent every day. She's going to want you to care about her."

"I already do," I replied in a frustrated voice. "I've cared since the moment I knew she existed."

I cared about a lot of people and a lot of things. I was simply an expert at reining in those emotions.

However, I knew I was going to have to change that particular trait. I just wasn't sure *how* to do it.

"Everything will be fine," she said reassuringly. "I'm going to tell Wren and my mother about the kidnapping the night before Wren leaves California. I'm also going to tell her that she's going to get to meet her father. I don't want to completely blindside her when she comes home. I will tell her that you participated in my rescue, but I won't mention Last Hope or your top-secret job. Those are your secrets to share when and if you want to do it. I know my daughter. She'd understand the need to keep those secrets quiet if you choose to tell her, but that's your decision, Colin."

"She'll probably have to know at some point," I mused. "I plan on being part of her life, and my life isn't normal. Hostage situations evolve quickly. They don't happen from nine-to-five. She's a smart girl. She's going to know that my life isn't normal, and I'm not going to lie to her."

"She's going to want to see the headquarters," Emma warned in a teasing tone. "If you have all of the high-tech equipment you've told me about, she'll be all over that."

"I'd take her there if she really wants to see it."

"I'd really like to see it myself," Emma said hesitantly. "I might not understand every piece of equipment, but I know that Last Hope is a big part of your life. You do important work there."

"I'll take you there," I answered in a heartbeat.

It suddenly hit me how much I wanted to share my life in California with Emma.

I was proud of everything we'd accomplished with Last Hope.

"You'll probably run into my partners and their wives," I added. "You know they're all involved as volunteers. I think you'd like all of them."

I'd already shared a lot about exactly how my billionaire partners' wives had gotten involved in Last Hope.

"They're younger than me, but I'm sure I'd like all of them."

"They're not that much younger," I countered. "And I think they'd want to pick your brain about raising kids. Wyatt is a mess right now because Shelby is pregnant."

Emma would be forty-six shortly, so she was a lot closer to their age than I was.

"He'll be fine once the baby is born," Emma said thoughtfully. "Pregnancy can be a crazy time. All I could think about was how to make sure I didn't screw up as a mother. It sounds like Wyatt is just worried about Shelby."

"He's obsessed," I told her drily. "I can't say that I blame him now. I wish I could have been there for you when you were pregnant, Emma."

"We can't change what happened in the past," she said gently.

Maybe not, but the thought of Emma pregnant, vulnerable, and alone made me completely insane.

"I had my mom," Emma explained. "She was so supportive. Once I got over the shock of being pregnant, I was happy. I was also glad that I'd never gotten pregnant with my ex. I turned myself inside out to make him happy, and I never could. I would have loved any child I had, but it would have been miserable with him. I blamed myself for my marriage failing and him turning to another woman because I wasn't able to get pregnant. I don't think I realized how ridiculous that was until we met. I had no concept of what a real man should be until we met in Virginia Beach. You might think that you're awkward with people, but you listened to me. You made me feel…important. That brief encounter made me feel like I was worthy of something better than I had in my marriage."

Anger flooded through me at the thought of anyone not treating Emma like she was the most incredible woman in the world.

I rolled her under me and searched her face. "Did he hit you, Em?" I asked hoarsely.

Fuck! I'd find the bastard if he had.

I didn't care how long ago that relationship had happened.

She shook her head slowly. "No. But the emotional abuse was probably worse than getting punched. He gaslighted me for years. By the time we divorced, I felt like everything that went wrong in our marriage was my fault. He was my first really serious relationship, so I was probably easily manipulated. I had very little relationship experience to compare it to. Our time together was short, but you showed me things I'd never experienced before."

"You are important, Emma," I growled. "Hell, I felt like the luckiest bastard in the world when you agreed to be with me for a while. He was a fucking idiot not to feel the same way."

She stroked my cheek lovingly. "He wasn't…you. He was a huge mistake that I didn't realize I'd made until we met. That short period of time together changed my whole perspective. Maybe we weren't together, but I was glad that you were Wren's father."

Hell, I was damn glad that she was my daughter, too.

"What can I do to make you understand that you're important to me?" I asked.

She smiled at me. "You're here with me right now even though everything else that's important in your life is in California. You want to know our daughter. Every single thing you do tells me that we matter to you, Colin. You don't have to prove anything to me. That relationship was a long time ago. I'm not that silly woman anymore. I moved on and I was grateful that I came to my senses. In the last fourteen years, I've never settled for anything less than the way you made me feel in Virginia Beach. I guess I just want you to know how significant that time together was for me, and how much it changed my life. We may have called it a fling, but it was pretty important in a lot of ways to me."

"Even though I got you pregnant and walked away?" I asked.

"That wasn't your fault. We both agreed to something very temporary. Getting pregnant wasn't something that was even in the realm of possibility for me. Wren was my miracle child, and I wouldn't change what happened for any reason."

"I'd change the fact that I just walked away," I said grumpily.

Fuck! That was and probably always would be the biggest regret in my life.

"It wasn't just you," she informed me. "I could have said something before you left, and I didn't. Let it go, Colin. We're here together now. I think I just got a second miracle in my life, and I'm not about to wallow in regret when I have you with me now. I want to take advantage of every second."

The last of the ice around my heart started to thaw.

She was right.

Emma and I *were* given a second chance, and I'd be damned if I was going to take that for granted.

Maybe I didn't believe in fate, but the chances of Emma and I actually crossing each other's paths again were beyond astronomical.

"Exactly how do you plan on taking advantage of every second?" I asked as I stared down at her beautiful face.

She pushed her hips up until she was wriggling against my aching cock.

"I think I'd like to take a shower so we can get sweaty together all over again," she said with a happy sigh.

Emma squealed as I rose from the bed, picked her up, and carried her toward the bathroom.

That sounded like a good idea to me.

From this day forward, I was going to make sure that my woman got *everything* she wanted and deserved.

CHAPTER 23

Emma

"I never thought I'd say this," Brock said to me several days later. "But Marshall is so different that I almost don't recognize him as the same guy I've known for years."

It was the day before Wren was due to arrive home, and we were having a barbecue at Colin's rental home.

Sara was working, but the guys had all managed to make it here for dinner.

The place might be within walking distance of my cottage, but the two houses were vastly different.

The rental home had a ton of space with four bedrooms.

It also boasted a sizable back yard with a large patio and a pool.

I watched Colin as he joked around about how to barbecue the steaks with Nate, Gage, and Seth in the distance.

I was lounging with Brock in large patio chairs underneath the umbrella for shade.

Colin and I *had* taken advantage of every moment we'd spent together.

I had to admit we'd spent our fair share of time together burning up the sheets, but we'd always spent some quality time together after work just being together.

I'd shown Colin more of Cherry Cove so he was completely familiar with the town.

We'd also spent some time exploring different things in Traverse City, the biggest city in Northern Michigan.

Granted, it wasn't a big city by national standards, but it was close to Cherry Cove and the place that most of us went to when we wanted more amenities.

I finally shot Brock a questioning gaze. "How has he changed?"

"He just laughed," he said like that was a miracle. "And he actually smiles, Emma. That's some crazy shit for Marshall. He seems almost… human."

"He cares more than anyone realizes," I told him. "I don't think any of you ever looked deep enough to recognize it."

Sometimes it seriously pissed me off that no one seemed to look deep enough to see the *real* Colin.

Brock held up a hand. "In our defense, I don't think any of us were brave enough to push him. Everyone who knows him has the highest level of respect for Marshall, but he's also intimidating. I think we just assumed that all he thought about was business and problem solving. It's pretty hard to see that he actually has a sense of humor."

"It's not that hard," I said in an astonished voice.

Okay, Colin acted like he was emotionless at times, but I could always see through that façade as his way of protecting himself.

Brock lifted a brow. "Maybe it isn't for you, but he doesn't let his guard down for people in general. He was a SEAL commander. Now he's the founder of Last Hope. I guess I should have realized that he had to care to take on those responsibilities, but I never did until you came back into his life. I think he's actually learned how to relax."

"He's always known how to relax," I explained. "He wasn't always all business when we met. There's a whole other side of him that very few people know. He may not be good in social situations sometimes, but he cares more than anyone I know. Maybe too much sometimes. He takes the responsibility of the whole world onto his shoulders sometimes."

Brock nodded. "I can agree with that. He's saved a lot of lives, but he never wants credit or accolades for that."

"I could say the same about you, Nate, Gage, and Seth," I reminded him.

Brock shrugged that off. "We have the skills. It's the right thing to do."

Sometimes it drove me crazy that none of the men in my life saw themselves as special even though they risked their lives and gave their free time regularly to help people who were in danger.

"Has it ever occurred to you that the four of you are a little intimidating to some people, too?" I questioned.

"No," Brock replied. "We're just four normal guys who have a different kind of hobby."

I snorted. All of them were far from normal. They were all gruff and physically intimidating. The few people who really knew them didn't see them that way, but most people gave the four men their space.

"A hobby that no one knows about because it's highly secretive and dangerous," I said.

"We were Delta, Emma. We've always kept secrets."

"Is Last Hope the reason why none of you have ever had a serious relationship?" I asked curiously.

"Nope," Brock told me. "I think being solo is just a way of life for all of us. There's probably not a woman in the world who would want to put up with any of us."

I knew that wasn't true.

Any woman would be lucky to hook up with my friends.

They might seem intimidating to some people, but there weren't any kinder or more caring men than these four guys.

It was more likely that they'd just never found women who could see beyond their bullshit.

I also suspected that they'd never met anyone more important to them than Last Hope.

I hadn't known exactly what they were doing when they disappeared before I knew about Last Hope, but I did know that they dropped everything when they needed to take off at a moment's notice.

"I think Marshall is nervous about meeting Wren," Brock observed.

I *knew* he was, but he didn't need to be. "I had a long talk with her and my mother earlier. I told them both about the kidnapping, and she's ecstatic that she's finally going to get to meet her father."

"He'll be good to her," Brock said. "He might be nervous, but he's just as excited to meet his daughter. As long as I've known him, he's never been the kind of guy to let anyone down. He's the most reliable person I know. He might be intimidating, but we've always trusted him with our lives."

"I trust him, too," I said confidently.

"You're crazy about him," he accused.

"Guilty," I answered happily.

Brock frowned. "I know he feels the same way. Exactly how is that going to work with you here in Michigan and him in California?"

I shook my head slowly. "We haven't really discussed the future. It's too early for that. He hasn't even met his daughter yet, and he's only been back in my life for a short time."

"He can't exactly move his headquarters, and even if he could, his partners' lives are in California. And your life is here with Wren."

"We aren't going to just dump each other after the summer is over," I said stubbornly.

Brock grinned. "I'm not saying that has to happen. It's just geography. I'm just saying that it's reality that you have separate lives in different states that are across the country from each other."

"I'm a mature woman," I informed him. "I realize that. I know it's not going to be easy when he has to go back to California."

Like it or not, Colin and I were going to have to deal with another separation.

It wasn't like he could just stay here and not deal with his life in California.

"We'll all be here for you when that has to happen," Brock said solemnly.

I swallowed a lump in my throat.

My four male friends had always been there for me when I'd had ups and downs in my life.

"Have I ever thanked you for being a protective friend?" I asked softly.

His grin widened. "Nope. As I recall, you have called me a pain in your ass once in a while."

"I never meant that," I blurted out. "Making me check in with you every day from Lania probably saved my life. You worrying about me probably saved my life, too."

If my friends hadn't been overprotective, I would have died before I'd had a chance to get rescued.

"You've always been there for us, too, Emma," Brock said seriously. "You befriended all of us without a second thought when we first got to Cherry Cove, and you've been there for us ever since. If we were sick, you were there. If we got injured, you were there. If you just thought we needed a friend, you were there. Worrying about you comes natural to us."

"I've always worried about the four of you, too," I told him honestly. "You scared the hell out of me when you just disappeared. I never really got used to that, but I knew that I couldn't force you to tell me what you were doing."

"Do you think we liked it?" Brock asked gruffly. "I felt guilty every time I saw the relieved look on your face when we got back. We wanted to tell you the truth, but we couldn't. When we signed up with Last Hope, we gave our word that we wouldn't tell anyone for the good of the organization. It's a huge relief for us that you know the truth now."

"I'm not sure that I'll worry less now that I know exactly what you're doing," I warned him.

I'd probably be more concerned now that I knew that they were going into dangerous situations to rescue hostages.

"At least you'll know exactly where we are and what we're doing," Brock answered. "We can tell you when we have to leave, and Marshall can let you know when we're coming home."

I'd always known that Brock, Nate, Gage, and Seth were incredible men, but I had to wonder if they really knew just how special they were for dedicating a large part of their lives to helping other people.

It wasn't their job or their duty to rescue hostages anymore, but they still took those responsibilities seriously.

I smiled at Brock. "I think I'm pretty lucky to call every one of you my friends."

"You're stuck with us," Brock said jokingly. "We might be a pain in your ass sometimes, but we've always been loyal pains in the asses. We care about you and Wren, but I have a feeling we're about to become secondary protectors now that Marshall is in the picture. He looks at you like he'd destroy anyone who tried to hurt you. I have a feeling he's going to feel the same way about his daughter."

I had to admit that Colin was protective.

"I think it's kind of sweet," I said with a sigh.

"Sweet?" Brock answered. "It's not sweet. It's fucking scary."

"Not to me," I informed him. "There isn't a single thing about Colin that scares me."

"I have to admit that it's kind of amusing to see one small woman handle a guy like Marshall the way you do," Brock replied.

I didn't manage Colin.

The stubborn man was completely unmanageable at times.

But he cared about me.

He listened to me.

He respected me.

"We're different," I admitted. "But for some reason, we're perfect for each other."

"You make him happy, Emma," Brock told me. "And I think he makes you happy, too. It doesn't matter how different you are. Hell, I think Marshall needs a woman like you in his life."

I wanted to tell him that all Colin needed was a woman who loved him and accepted him exactly the way he was.

I knew that because I craved exactly the same thing.

I stayed quiet as we rose to go join the rest of the group.

When and if Colin was ready, he was going to be the first one to know exactly how I felt.

CHAPTER 24

Marshall

I paced my rental place the next afternoon, staring at the gifts I'd bought for Wren every time I passed by the dining room table. The table was full.

Emma had pitched a fit over those gifts, but I'd gotten them anyway. Twenty-six gifts total.

Thirteen for every one of her birthdays I'd missed, and thirteen for every Christmas I'd missed in my daughter's life.

I thought it was a logical number.

Since I already knew that my daughter had a gift for technology, I'd gotten her things that would challenge her brain.

The rest of the stuff I'd picked up because Emma had mentioned that they were some of Wren's favorite things.

I wasn't trying to buy her affection.

I'd just picked up a gift for every occasion I regretted missing in her life so far.

I glanced at my watch for the millionth time in the last thirty minutes.

Emma had picked up Wren around lunchtime.

She'd said she was going to feed Wren and bring her over as soon as they got settled into the cottage.

The three of us were going to walk to town and get an ice cream. The ice cream shop had been around for decades. Emma and I had gone there together, and I had to admit that they had the best soft serve ice cream cones I'd ever tasted.

It's just a damn ice cream. It's not a big deal.

While my rational mind tried to make me see some reason, my irrational mind was winning this particular battle.

What if she didn't like me?

What if my injured leg and significant limp bothered her?

What if she resented the fact that I hadn't been around for the last thirteen years?

Hell, she didn't even know what I looked like.

Emma and I had never taken pictures in Virginia Beach, so she hadn't even seen a photo of me.

I might be her biological father, but I was going to be a complete stranger to Wren.

I grimaced and stopped prowling around the house when the doorbell finally rang.

You can't expect to be a father to her right now. Just try to be her friend.

I was determined to be exactly that when I opened the door.

However, those expectations flew out of my head the moment I saw Emma and Wren on my doorstep.

Emma had told me that Wren had experienced a significant growth spurt recently.

She wasn't as tall as her mother, but she was only a few inches shorter.

The moment I locked eyes with my daughter I felt like those solemn gray eyes so much like my own were looking into my fucking soul.

Wren was like a female mirror image of me, and I felt completely gut punched.

Yeah, I'd seen her picture, but I'd had no idea exactly how I'd feel looking back at her in person.

This was *my* child, and every protective instinct in my body suddenly flared to life.

Her brown hair barely touched her shoulders, and my daughter wasn't smiling like her mother was at the moment.

She looked at me like she was trying to figure me out, and I was silent because I had no idea what to say.

I wasn't sure how long we stayed like that, our eyes locked, our gazes steady, but I frowned as I saw her bottom lip start to tremble.

"Dad?" she said uncertainly.

The moment that word came out of my daughter's mouth, I knew I was completely fucked.

"Wren?" I said huskily.

Without another word, Wren launched her smaller body toward me, and I caught her as she landed against my chest.

I closed my eyes and simply held my girl.

I hadn't expected this kind of reception, but I was damn grateful for it.

She'd accepted me in a nanosecond like she'd instantly recognized me as her father.

I sure as hell had never had someone who just accepted who I was in a heartbeat and thoroughly embraced it.

I wasn't used to it.

It wasn't normal for me.

But I savored every second of that enthusiastic hug from my child.

It was humbling for me, and I wasn't a humble guy.

I felt like my heart was about to explode by the time she finally stepped back.

"We look so much alike," Wren observed as she looked me over thoroughly and finally smiled.

"You definitely have your mother's smile and some of her features," I said as I let the two of them step inside.

Emma looked beautiful in her summer top and shorts.

Wren was dressed in a pair of jeans and cropped T-shirt.

We seated ourselves in the living room.

Wren sat on the couch beside me and turned to look at me again like she couldn't stop staring.

I was pretty certain that I was probably still staring at her in awe like an idiot.

I cleared my throat before I spoke. "Before we say anything else, I want you to know that I would have been there for you and your mom if I'd known about you, Wren."

She cocked her head in an adorable way that made me want to hug her all over again. "I know about all that," she said dismissively. "I don't care. You didn't know, and it wasn't your fault. You know now and you're here. Mom said you're intellectually gifted like me. I want to know about your life. What things are like for you in California. I want to know about what it was like to be a SEAL commander. I guess I just want to know everything."

And just like that...Wren blew off everything I'd missed out on in the past and focused on the present.

Hell, maybe that was easier to do when you were a kid.

Honestly, that action was so much like her mother that it shouldn't have surprised me.

"I'm not going to promise that I'll be a perfect father in the future. I've never had a child, so I have zero practice at being a parent," I warned her. "But I'll always be there if you need me."

She shrugged. "Being there is enough. I probably won't be an ideal daughter, either. I've never had a dad. But I'd like to. Maybe you can help me feel more normal even though I'm gifted."

I had to swallow the enormous lump in my throat before I spoke. "I probably never thought of my intelligence as a gift. I don't remember a time when I didn't think differently than other people my age."

"I think some people think I'm odd," Wren said without an ounce of rancor about that fact.

"You're not odd," I said defensively. "You're smart. You'll appreciate that a lot more as you get older. If people can't appreciate that your mind just works a little differently, that's their issue. There's not a single thing wrong with you, Wren."

She smiled at me and my heart melted. "I know. Mom always makes sure that I know that I'm just unique. I used to think that was bad because I didn't fit in, but I don't feel that way so much anymore. I met some other kids in San Diego last summer that are gifted, so I know I'm not the only kid in the world who doesn't always fit in."

"Did you see them this summer?" Emma asked.

Wren nodded enthusiastically. "They're all in a specific program at school for gifted kids, so they all hang out together. I like being with them. I feel like we're all part of the same tribe."

"We don't have those programs at our local school," Emma told me regretfully. "I wish we did."

"I like my friends here," Wren said. "We just don't think the same way. Some of them are starting to get obsessed with boys. I'd usually rather talk about solving some of the major social issues we have in the world right now."

I grinned because she said that like the very thought of boys was absolutely disgusting to her.

Hell, she *was* at that age when some girls had enormous crushes on the opposite sex.

Personally, I was damn glad she wasn't showing that much interest in the opposite sex yet.

In my eyes, Wren was *still* a child.

I wasn't sure it was preferable for a kid to be thinking about poverty, racism, and food insecurity, but it was probably better than being obsessed with boys.

"I bought you a few things," I told Wren.

"A few things?" Emma said drily. "You bought her a ridiculous amount of gifts."

"Twenty-six," I confirmed.

Wren looked at me for a moment before she said, "Thirteen and thirteen. One for each Christmas and birthday that we weren't together."

"Exactly," I confirmed.

Okay, it was a little unnerving that my kid understood my logic so well, but she *was* my daughter, and her brain obviously worked similarly to mine.

"It makes sense," Wren told me. "But you didn't have to do that. You didn't know about me then."

"I wanted to," I said simply.

"What are they?" she asked with the excitement of a kid in her voice.

Wren was pretty unique.

As Emma had mentioned, she still had the emotional development of girls her age, but an intelligence that was probably scary to most people.

But I wasn't most people.

I was her father, and I understood her perfectly.

I nodded my head toward the dining room. "They're all on the table in the dining room."

Wren looked at her mother. "Can I go for a few minutes?"

Emma nodded. "You're going to need more than a few minutes to open all of that stuff."

Wren shot me a huge smile as she leaned over and kissed my cheek. "Thanks, Dad. I'll be back."

My gut wrenched as my girl wandered off to the dining room.

Christ! So this was what it was like to have a daughter.

I knew I was going to worry about her welfare and her happiness for the rest of my fucking life, and I'd only known her for a matter of minutes.

It was going to be pure hell, but I knew I didn't want to miss a single moment of that torture in the future.

CHAPTER 25

Emma

Wren and I were as close as a mother and daughter could possibly be, but it warmed my heart every time I watched her with her father.

We'd all been together every afternoon and evening for the last week, and I felt like I was watching two peas in a pod whenever I saw or heard them interact.

I knew that Wren was a lot like me because I'd raised her, but there were traits that she had that were so similar to Colin's that it made me smile.

I had to stop Colin at times from spoiling her rotten, but I knew that Wren would never take his generosity for granted.

She was a thoughtful kid, and she was thriving from her father's attention.

He'd planned some kind of summer activity every day, but I could tell that he'd enjoyed anything he did with me and Wren.

He was slowly settling into his role as a father, and I was glad that Wren had another parent she could talk to about her overactive intelligence.

I had never suggested or asked her to call him *Dad*.

In her typical Wren behavior, she'd just decided it was the logical thing to call him.

I let out a long sigh and rolled onto my back in the bed.

We were spending the night at Colin's place because we were leaving fairly early for the Detroit Zoo in the morning.

Wren loved the place, but we hadn't been there in ages.

Staying here at Colin's place tonight had been Wren's idea because we were leaving so early in the morning, and I couldn't refuse. She didn't have a lot of the summer left, and I understood that she wanted to spend as much time with her father as possible.

Colin had taken us out for dinner earlier to celebrate my birthday.

He'd helped Wren buy me some perfume from her, and he'd bought me a ridiculously expensive gift that I loved.

I wasn't sure how he'd managed to purchase the beautiful art deco bracelet he'd given me, but judging by the quality of the antique piece, it had been pricey.

Probably just as pricey as the necklace he'd given me fourteen years ago.

The stubborn man had blown off the expensive gift like it was insignificant, but I knew I was going to cherish that piece of jewelry for the rest of my life.

Go to sleep, Emma, and stop thinking about Colin.

I wanted to do exactly that, but it was hard not to think about him when we were in the same house.

Wren had chosen the bedroom upstairs, but I was downstairs.

In the bedroom next to *his*.

I was happy that he was getting to know his daughter, but I really missed the two of us being in the same bed.

We'd had a few stolen kisses when Wren wasn't close by, but we'd been careful.

She needed some time to adjust to having a father.

But the sudden separation from Colin was killing me.

You'll live, Emma. Just go to sleep!

I let out a huff of frustration and fluffed my pillow.

I was still wide awake, and I probably wasn't sleeping anytime soon.

I was a little startled when my bedroom door suddenly opened and Colin strode into the room in his boxer briefs.

He didn't say a word.

He simply picked me up and headed back toward the door.

"Colin?" I whispered. "What are you doing?"

"Making sure I don't have to spend another night without you," he grumbled as he entered his room, closed the door with his foot, and dropped me gently onto his bed.

"Wren…" I stuttered.

"She'll never know," he said as he took off his boxer briefs. "I'll make sure you're back in your own bed by sunrise. I just checked on her upstairs. She's out cold. I'm tired of pretending that I don't want you in my bed, Emma."

My breath caught as I saw his fully erect cock.

He'd obviously been thinking about this for a while now.

Just like I'd been doing restlessly next door.

Wanting him so badly that I couldn't sleep.

"I missed you," he said grumpily as he headed toward the bed.

I smiled as I quickly undressed and tossed my nightgown and panties on the floor. "I missed you, too."

I let out a sigh of relief as his lips met mine, and he pinned me to the bed with his massive body.

He felt so damn good that a sharp, aching need shot through my body and directly between my thighs.

I tried to stifle it, but a raw moan escaped from my lips as soon as he released my mouth.

"Fuck me, Colin," I pleaded as I lifted my hips.

I wanted him inside me.

No fanfare.

No foreplay.

I'd been thinking about this for a week, and the foreplay wasn't necessary right now.

"I don't think I have the patience to do anything else right now," he rumbled as his lips skimmed over my neck.

I wrapped my arms around his neck and lifted my hips again.

He grabbed my ass and thrust inside me with a ferocity that took my breath away.

"Yes," I hissed as I wrapped my legs tightly around him.

This was exactly what I needed.

This kind of intimacy.

This kind of intensity.

The pure sensuality that flowed between the two of us.

His thrusts were slow and hard, and meant to drive me completely insane.

He ground against me, stimulating my clit with every forward motion.

"Colin," I whispered in a sensual voice that I barely recognized as my own.

He rolled and pulled me on top of him. "Ride me, Em," he said in a husky, tormented voice. "Take what you need. This isn't going to last long for me."

I kept up the same pace and rhythm as I looked into his desperate, wild, and utterly gorgeous gray eyes.

My heart stuttered as I realized that he was giving me complete control.

He'd never done that before.

He wanted to make sure I was satisfied because *he* was on the edge.

Colin trusted me, and that knowledge made my heart flutter inside of my chest.

He wasn't a man who gave up control to anyone easily.

I did exactly what he wanted, and I savored every stroke of his cock as I rode him until I was exhausted and sweaty.

I squeaked as he roughly rolled me onto my back again.

"Fucking hell, woman," he rasped beside my ear. "Are you trying to kill me?"

"No," I panted as I wrapped my arms around his neck. "I'm trying to get enough of you, but I can't."

"I'll never get enough of you, either, and that scares the hell out of me sometimes," he said hoarsely.

I knew the moment his patience finally snapped.

He took my wrists, pinned them beside my head, and fucked me with an intensity that started to send me over the edge.

"You're mine, Emma," he said in a commanding voice. "Say it before I completely lose it."

"Yours," I said with a small moan that I couldn't contain.

I'd always been Colin's.

And he'd always been mine.

My heart had probably always known that even though my brain had rejected it for years.

My core clenched hard around his cock, and my climax consumed me.

I had to bite my lip to keep from screaming his name.

I let go completely, trusting this man that I loved to catch me when I finally fell back to Earth.

Colin followed me over the edge, but he did catch me, and then he rolled and pulled me on top of him.

"You need to stay here more often," Colin said in a graveled voice. "I'm not sure I can stay out of your bed this long again."

I didn't want to be separated from him, either.

I had no idea what we were going to do when we were across the country from each other.

"Maybe you should invite us to spend the night more often," I suggested as I ran my hand down his chest.

"You can stay here every damn night," he grumbled. "I want you here, Emma."

I laughed. "Do you want me to pack our stuff and move Wren and me into your place?" I teased.

"Yes," he said in a completely serious tone.

He sounded so disgruntled that I stroked my hand over his jaw soothingly.

The two of us were in a totally hopeless situation at the moment, and it was wearing on me, too.

Wren would be going back to school soon, and Colin couldn't stay in Cherry Cove forever.

His entire life was in California, and he'd already stayed way longer than he'd initially planned.

"I'll tell Wren that we can stay here until she starts school," I offered.

"I'm pacified," he agreed. "For now."

I snuggled against him. "For now?"

"I meant what I said, Emma. This isn't going to be over for us. Even when I have to go back to California. I do have to get back to California because I have responsibilities there, but this isn't over. We're not over."

Tears filled my eyes. "I don't want it to be over."

Colin and I had walked away from each other once.

Now that he was back in my life, I knew it would shatter my heart to do it all over again.

CHAPTER 26

Marshall

"You're actually hacking into a site," Wren accused in an awed voice close to my ear early the next morning.

I slammed my laptop closed and turned to see my daughter leaning over my shoulder while I was working.

Fuck! What was she doing up at this hour? Didn't teenagers usually sleep late?

It was barely daylight.

I'd carried a sleeping Emma back to her bed a short time ago as promised and had decided to work for a while.

The majority of Nick's enemies had been apprehended, but we both knew there was one more that needed to be caught. There was someone higher up that had to be discovered, and I'd find that bastard eventually.

"I was," I said cautiously as my daughter flopped onto the couch in her pajamas.

I'd promised myself that I'd never lie to Wren unless absolutely necessary.

Hell, I'd probably have a difficult time lying to Wren even if I wanted to do it because she was too damn smart.

Her mind was always working and reasoning things out.

"Why?" she asked curiously. "I know it's tempting to challenge yourself, but after I got in trouble for hacking I had to stop. It took a while to get caught, but you'll probably get caught if you keep doing it. Mom was really mad at me. She'd probably be mad at you, too, if she finds out."

"I won't get caught," I said as I released a frustrated breath. "I'm not doing it for the challenge, Wren."

Hell, I should have known that my kid was trying to hack into websites just because she could.

"Then why are you doing it?" she asked, pinning me with a curious gaze.

"Because it's part of my job," I explained in a resigned tone. "I gather intel for the government as a contractor. I can't tell you a lot about my job because it's classified. I'd prefer that no one else knows about it."

"Does Mom know?" she questioned.

I nodded. "She's the only person who knows. Now you know, too."

"I'd never tell anyone," she replied. "But I wish I could ask questions about it."

I trusted my daughter. She was intelligent enough to realize why secrecy was important.

"You can't," I said flatly. "I just want you to know that I'm not hacking for nefarious reasons or for the challenge. Your mother was right to be mad at you. Hacking is wrong unless you have a good reason for doing it."

"If you work for the government, you must be really good at it. Did you do it when you were a SEAL commander?" she asked as she sent me an admiring glance.

"Not very often," I answered. "But I learned a lot when I was in the Navy. We had an intelligence department that gave us most of our data. It was my job to oversee missions."

She sent me a probing look. "You didn't just oversee them. You were there. That's how you injured your leg. It happened doing a mission."

I shot her a surprised look. Wren knew about my history, but I'd never shared many of the details because it wasn't something a kid needed to know. "How do you know that?"

My daughter rolled her eyes adorably. "It doesn't take a genius to figure that out. You're still doing some kind of hostage rescue. I heard you talking to Wyatt about one the other day. How is that possible?"

I let out an exasperated breath.

I had been talking to Wyatt two days ago about a mission he'd needed to run in my absence. The operation had gone well, but he'd briefed me on the situation and we'd discussed everything right before the mission had been completed.

While I was proud of my daughter's inquisitive, intelligent brain, there were a few downsides to having a gifted kid.

Hell, was there anything my daughter didn't notice and analyze?

I gave up and told her the basics about Last Hope, including the information about her mother's kidnapping and her subsequent rescue.

It would be more confusing to Wren to not know the truth at this point.

"Seriously?" she said excitedly when I'd finished the explanation. "That's what Brock, Nate, Gage, and Seth do when they take off without an explanation for a while? I've always known that they were Delta, but I never suspected that. I know Wyatt, but I don't know the rest of your partners in San Diego."

"You'll meet them someday," I promised her.

"Can I see your headquarters?" she asked.

I grinned at her. Emma had warned me about this. "If you want to see it, I'll take you there. I trust you. I think you can keep my secrets."

"Of course I'll keep your secrets," she answered. "I know it's important, and you're my dad."

For Wren, keeping my secrets was just that simple.

Seeing that earnest, adoring look on her face made my gut ache.

I still wasn't quite used to having a daughter who cared about me unconditionally simply because I was her father.

Wren would care about me unless I gave her a very good reason not to do it.

I happened to like her affection, so I wasn't about to do anything to jeopardize her trust in me as a father.

Emma had always said that Wren was her miracle child, but she was my miracle kid, too.

A daughter I never even dreamed of having.

Both Emma and Wren brought out protective instincts I'd never even known that I had.

Emma was *mine*.

Wren was *my* daughter.

There wasn't a damn thing I wouldn't do to keep both of them safe and happy.

Wren asked several more questions about Last Hope, and I answered what I could as honestly as possible.

She was curious about the world, and she pondered social issues and unpleasant things that most girls didn't at her age.

It would probably never be possible to shield her from everything unpleasant that happened in the world because she made it her business to know about all of them.

I'd quickly discovered that she could still be a kid and wonder about things that only adults usually thought about.

I understood that because I was very much the same at her age.

I was going to do my damnedest to make sure she tried to stay focused on the fun kids were having at her age, but there would be times when her brain wanted to go other places.

I knew I couldn't just stifle her questions and pretend that those questions didn't matter because they were unpleasant things to talk about.

She let out a contented sigh once I'd answered her questions.

"You and Mom slept together last night," Wren stated. "Do you want to be together?"

The hopeful look in my daughter's eyes nearly killed me.

I raised a brow. "How do you know that?"

She shrugged. "I woke up in the middle of the night. I was hungry. Her door was open, but she wasn't in her room when I came downstairs."

Okay, we were busted. What in the hell was I supposed to tell my daughter?

I decided honesty was the best answer.

"It's complicated, Wren," I said carefully.

"Maybe I don't like boys," she explained. "But I know about sex and relationships. I'm a teenager. I had sex ed last year."

"They do that in junior high?" I asked, surprised.

She nodded. "I'm going into high school, Dad. I'm not a child anymore."

Sometimes I had to wonder if my daughter was ever really a child. Still, she was only thirteen…

"I care about your mom, Wren, and she cares about me."

How did a guy keep things simple enough for a teenager to understand?

"Then why can't you just be together?" she asked.

Fuck! I could really use Emma's calming, motherly presence right now.

I was an amateur at this whole fatherhood thing.

"You and your mother's lives are here in Cherry Cove. My life is in San Diego."

"It's not *that* complicated," she reasoned. "It's not like we live in a different country. We could move to San Diego so we would be with you. I could get into the gifted program there in high school. Grandma is there, and I have friends there."

"You'd want to do that?" I asked hoarsely. "Just like that?"

She nodded enthusiastically. "Just like that."

"Wouldn't you miss your friends and your school?"

Something that felt a lot like hope started to form in my gut.

"A little," she admitted. "But I like my friends there, too, and I don't like the winters here. It's cold and depressing. I'd happily trade what I have here to be with you all the time. I don't want you to go. We just found each other."

My gut wrenched when I saw my daughter's lower lip start to quiver and tears fill those gray eyes that were so much like my own.

There was my girl.

She might act like a mini adult sometimes, but those adolescent emotions were still there.

I got my ass up from the recliner, sat next to my daughter, and hugged her.

She wrapped her arms around me and hugged me back so tightly that I could barely breathe.

Hell, I'd happily suffocate if that was what my girl needed.

I kissed the top of her head. "Adulthood sucks sometimes, Wren. I don't want to go, but I have responsibilities in California. We have to make hard choices that aren't always easy. I want your mom to be happy, too."

Maybe that wasn't the appropriate thing to say, but it was the truth.

My daughter finally released me and stared at me solemnly.

"I know that," she said tearfully. "I think Mom has thought about moving to San Diego, but it's expensive there. She's been trying to save for my college expenses, but I think I could get a job in another year."

"Not happening," I said flatly. "You're going to focus on your education. I'll take care of all of your expenses. I'm your father."

She frowned. "It's going to be expensive. I want to get my doctorate. I want to be a marine scientist."

I knew that. Wren and I had discussed it several times.

My daughter was already certified as a junior scuba diver, and her mother had gotten her adult certification, too.

Seth was a dive instructor, and they'd both gotten certified as soon as Wren was eligible for a junior diver certification.

One of the main reasons we were going to the zoo today was to visit the penguinarium at the Detroit Zoo. The zoo had the largest penguin exhibit in the world.

My daughter loved everything marine wildlife, but she was fascinated by the penguins in particular.

"You don't need to worry about the expense," I assured her as I awkwardly used my T-shirt to wipe a tear away from her cheek. "You'll get your education."

Christ! She was *still* a kid.

And I hated to see my girl cry.

It tore my guts out that she was crying over not seeing *me* every day.

"I want to see you every day, too, Wren, but that may not be possible for us right now. But we'll be together as often as possible. I'll come here, and you can come to San Diego whenever you have time off from school."

I'd move Emma and my daughter to San Diego in a heartbeat if I thought Emma would be happy there. But the fact that Emma had never even suggested it was telling me it would be a no-go for her.

One thing I'd never wanted to do was step on Emma's toes as a mother.

She'd done a phenomenal job of raising Wren here in Cherry Cove all by herself as a single parent.

I never wanted to say anything to suggest that she'd been anything but a fantastic parent.

Yeah, I'd put my foot down about paying expenses, but Emma had been Wren's parent for thirteen years.

I'd been a father to my daughter for a matter of weeks.

I couldn't and I wouldn't tell her where and how to raise my daughter.

Those were her decisions to make as Wren's primary parent.

Yeah, I wanted Emma and Wren to move to California, but it *had* to be Emma who made that suggestion so she didn't feel like she was being pressured to move because that's what I wanted.

If that was something Emma was considering on her own, she would have mentioned it by now.

Hell, she'd spent most of her life in Cherry Cove, and she was happy here with her friends and with the life she'd built here.

What I'd said to Wren was true. I *did* want Emma to be happy. Asking her to start her life all over again in California was way too much to ask. Going from small town Michigan to big city California was night and day different.

"Your mom is going to bring some of your things over so the two of you can stay here with me until you have to go back to school," I told Wren. "We can spend more time together that way."

My daughter's eyes brightened. "Really?"

I nodded. "Really. I'm always going to want to spend as much time with you as possible."

"Are you and Mom going to sleep together?" she asked. "I think you should. You care about each other."

I coughed because I wasn't quite sure how to answer that question.

"We'll see," I said noncommittally.

Personally, I'd prefer not to hide the way I felt about Emma, but that was a decision her mother needed to make.

Wren wrapped her arms around me again and hugged me. "I'm glad we're going to stay here. I love you, Dad."

I wrapped my arms around my girl as her words completely broke me.

"I love you, too, Wren," I told her, knowing I'd always love and adore my daughter until the day I took my last breath.

I didn't care if I was completely screwed.

She'd wrapped her fingers around a heart I hadn't known existed until recently, and I didn't ever want her to let it go.

CHAPTER 27

Emma

I let out a happy sigh a week later as I relaxed in a lounge chair on the deck of Seth's boat.

So much had changed between Colin and I over the last week.

As promised, we'd stayed at his place.

The two of us no longer hid the fact that we wanted to be together, and Wren had encouraged that by pushing us together as much and as often as possible.

I wasn't blind to my daughter's motivations.

She wanted her mother and father to be together, and she made no attempt to hide those not-so-subtle attempts to make that happen.

Wren completely adored and idolized her father.

I suspected this probably wouldn't *always* be the case.

The two of them were too much alike, and there were bound to be times when they butted heads in the future.

But I had no doubt that Wren was always going to love Colin, whether they disagreed or not.

They got closer and closer every single day.

I was starting to dread the following week when Wren would have to go back to school.

Colin would have to leave for California.

I knew that he was determined to continue his relationship with Wren and me, and I was just as determined not to lose him, but I wondered how the distance would affect all of us.

My heart ached at the thought of being separated from Colin.

We'd spent the last week together almost constantly.

And I'd spent every night in his bed.

The three of us spent our days together, but Colin and I spent our nights indulging in very adult things.

I wished it could stay the same forever, but that just wasn't possible for the two of us.

I was going to have to learn how to do a long-distance relationship.

We'd see each other as much as possible, and he'd spend as much time with Wren as he could.

It wasn't what my heart wanted to happen, but it was the only thing we could do.

Colin couldn't possibly move to Cherry Cove, even if he didn't mind leaving San Diego. The Last Hope headquarters was in San Diego, and Colin had dedicated a lot of his life to helping those hostages and building that organization.

Wren had mentioned that she wouldn't mind living in San Diego, but Colin had never even mentioned the possibility of us moving there.

It knew it was too soon to even think about that, and I had to keep my priorities straight.

I couldn't afford a home in San Diego, so I hadn't even brought up the possibility of moving.

I didn't want to feel like I was pressuring Colin into more than what we had before we were both ready.

Maybe I was ready, but he was still adjusting to being a father, and he'd never been in a committed relationship before.

It wasn't like I could just move into his place at this point in our relationship.

We'd have to rent, and the rents were pretty outrageous there compared to Michigan.

After living in our cottage in Cherry Cove, Wren would probably hate having an apartment in a big city.

We weren't struggling anymore in Cherry Cove, but things would be tight for me in San Diego.

I didn't want to do that to Wren.

Granted, Colin had already put an eye-popping amount of money into Wren's educational savings. So much that I'd never have to worry about her educational expenses again.

However, I was her mother and I'd always paid for my daughter's normal expenses.

I was fine with him paying for her college education because he'd insisted on it, and I was okay with him covering some of Wren's expenses, but he'd had this fatherhood situation thrust on him unexpectedly.

I wasn't about to take his money so I could live in San Diego.

We'd talked more extensively about finances, and Colin's wealth had surprised me, but I wasn't going to take advantage of the fact that he had a lot of money.

I didn't want his money.

I just wanted…him.

I'd love him no matter what his financial circumstances might be.

"You look like you're pretty deep in thought," Brock observed from the captain's chair of the boat.

I snapped out of my thoughts. "Sorry," I said sheepishly.

I *had* been completely ignoring Brock's presence for a while.

He was manning the boat while Seth, Colin, and Wren were diving. I'd opted out of the diving today to stay on the boat.

We'd been running to fun places day after day, and I was little tired.

I liked to dive, but I knew that Wren was safe with Colin and Seth. I wasn't the expert divers that they were anyway.

Seth had always been extremely safety conscious with Wren, but Colin had taken the pre-dive stuff to a whole different level.

He'd checked Wren's gear several times after Seth had already done it, and he'd reminded our daughter of every safety rule in existence before they'd gone down a few minutes ago.

Wren had dived this particular shipwreck before.

It was shallow enough to stay within her depth limits as a junior diver, but Colin had fussed over her anyway, which I'd found completely adorable.

My daughter had patiently listened to everything that her father said even though Seth had gone over all of those things a million times before.

"Are you worried about Wren?" Brock asked.

I shook my head. I always worried a little about my daughter when she was diving, but I was used to that. "She's safe with Colin and Seth."

"Very safe," he agreed. "They're both instructors and Marshall was a SEAL. He's been diving most of his life."

"The waves are getting a little choppy," I noticed.

It had been perfectly calm when they'd gone down a few minutes ago, but the waves were starting to kick up.

"Yeah," he commented. "I noticed that. Things can change out here in a matter of moments. It doesn't look like it's about to storm, but the winds have shifted a little. Lake Michigan weather is a bitch sometimes."

"You should be used to that by now," I teased.

While Gage was the only native Michigander, the rest of the guys had been here for years. Long enough to know just how fast the weather could change on the Great Lakes.

"I'm used to it," he grumbled. "But that doesn't mean that I always like it."

"You love it here," I said. "Even the winters."

All of the guys thrived during the Michigan winters because they loved winter sports just as much as they liked the summer ones.

"Most of the time," he admitted. "But I could do without some of the crazy storms, especially if I already have plans to do something on the water."

You had to learn to roll with the weather on the Great Lakes, and Grand Traverse Bay was part of Lake Michigan.

Cherry Cove had its fair share of nasty summer storms and lake-effect snow in the winter that seemed like it would never stop.

I was a Michigander so I was used to the fact that the weather could change quickly, especially when you lived on the lake.

"That's Seth," Brock said in a surprised voice as a head popped out of the water in the distance. "Why in the hell did he surface? I don't see Wren or Marhsall."

I stood up and leaned over the railing.

Seth was swimming like lightning toward his boat.

My eyes searched the water frantically for my daughter and Colin, but they were nowhere in sight.

When Seth pulled himself onto the boat, his expression was grim.

"Wren got caught up in a current. Marshall signaled for me to surface and call for help. He went after her," he said solemnly as he sprinted to the captain's area.

I watched as Seth called the authorities on the radio, my heart pounding inside my chest.

Wren was in trouble.

The currents in Lake Michigan could be brutal sometimes.

Wren knew what to do, but she was still a kid.

"I need to go down," I said in a panic.

"No!" Brock said as he wrapped an arm around my shoulders. "I know your instinct is to go after your daughter, but you're a novice diver, Emma. You going down there right now could cause even more problems."

I looked up at Brock's pleading gaze.

He was trying to make me see sense, but I was Wren's mother.

I knew he was right, but I couldn't let go of the instinct to rescue my child.

"Marshall is with her, Emma. He'll bring her back," Seth said firmly after he'd radioed for help. "Wren is a junior diver, but she's the most competent junior diver I've ever worked with. Marshall's diving skills blow every other diver out of the water. He'll find her. We need to try to figure out where they ended up and find his emergency surface marker buoy. I imagine that the Coast Guard will be here to help us shortly. Don't panic on me now, Emma. You know what we have to do, and you know that Marshall would die himself before he'd let anything happen to his daughter."

I nodded slowly.

I had to pull myself together.

Freaking out wasn't going to help my daughter or Colin right now.

"You drive," I said. "Brock and I will search the water for the buoy."

Brock squeezed my shoulders as Seth fired up the boat.

"You trust Marshall, Emma. Trust him to bring your daughter home."

"I do trust him," I said as tears rolled down my cheeks. "But he's not superhuman. There are limits to what he can do against the currents."

People died every year on Lake Michigan from the lake currents. They could be brutal and deadly.

They weren't static, and Seth could only make a guess as to where my daughter and Colin would eventually pop up.

"He's probably as close to superhuman as you're going to get," Brock answered as we moved to get into position to search the surface.

The two of us moved apart so we could see different areas and get a good view.

My hands were shaking as I gripped the railing, but I kept reassuring myself that Colin *would* do everything possible to save our daughter.

CHAPTER 28

Marshall

One moment I'd been beside my daughter exploring the exterior of the shipwreck.

A nanosecond later, she been swept away from my side.

Every reaction after that had been automatic.

I'd been diving most of my life, and I'd run into almost every conceivable emergency.

But there wasn't a damn thing that could have prepared me for losing sight of my young daughter under the water.

I'd motioned to Seth on autopilot to go call for help, and then I'd allowed the current to carry me in the same direction as my daughter.

It hadn't been a particularly strong current, but it had been enough to sweep Wren away because it had probably taken her by surprise.

Fuck! It had been incredibly calm when we'd entered the water.

Relief flooded over me as the current started to dissipate and I saw Wren struggling at the bottom of the lake.

She'd somehow ended up wrapped in a shitload of rope that was coming from an anchor at the lake bottom.

Thank fuck that she hadn't gone into a full-blown diver panic and ripped herself out of her gear.

I'd seen diver panic. When a diver got disoriented, it could lead to potentially erratic and irrational behavior.

I grabbed Wren by the shoulders and forced her to look at me.

Her eyes were wide, and I knew she was a little confused, but she stopped struggling frantically with the rope around her body.

I flashed her the diver's sign for *okay*, hoping she'd understand that everything was going to be alright.

She slowly nodded and let me work on getting her free from the rope.

As I slowly untangled the rope from her body, I could understand why she'd been struggling.

Her arms were almost immobilized, and she couldn't really kick with her legs tangled up in the heavy rope.

She *was* going to be alright.

We had plenty of air.

And I'd get her loose.

But I still couldn't quite let go of the sheer horror I'd experienced at the thought of my daughter drowning under my watch.

Wren was a good diver, but she was still a kid, and a junior diver.

She hadn't been exposed to some of the crazy shit that could happen to a diver.

Seth had been extremely careful with Wren, but what had just happened was proof that things could happen even when a diver was cautious.

Wren looked relieved when she was finally free of the rope.

I flashed her the *okay* sign again, and she immediately sent it back to me.

I released an emergency sausage to the surface so Wren and I could be found easier and wrapped my arms around my daughter's body.

I wasn't fucking letting her go again.

I didn't think we'd been swept that far away from the boat, so I started propelling the two of us to the surface.

Both of us removed our mouthpieces the moment we surfaced.

"That was kind of scary," Wren said, keeping her hand on my shoulder.

Fear was still clawing at my gut, and my daughter thought the experience was kind of scary?

"I know I panicked a little," she said woefully. "I think I was a little disoriented. I didn't understand why I couldn't move."

"That wasn't a little scary, Wren," I ground out. "It was fucking terrifying for me."

I usually watched my language around Wren, but the words had come out of my mouth before I could stop them.

"Why?" she asked. "You're an expert diver, and the current wasn't horrible."

"I wasn't worried about *me*," I said angrily. "I was worried about *you*."

Fuck! If I never saw Wren in danger again, it would be too damn soon.

"I'm okay, Dad," she said in a calm voice.

"Yeah, well, I'm not," I rasped as I looked around for the boat. "You could have died down there after you got tangled up in that anchor rope. And there are worse emergencies and a hell of a lot stronger currents that could have carried you away."

"We don't dive when the weather is bad or when there's a possibility of bad currents."

"We were careful today, and look what happened," I replied harshly.

"It was a freak accident," she argued. "What were the chances of me getting tangled up in that rope?"

"I don't care. No more scuba diving. Ever. You might be smart, but you're still a kid."

"You're being unreasonable," Wren said.

Hell, I knew that, but I couldn't stop myself.

I wasn't about to see Wren in any kind of danger again.

"Whoa!" she said as she looked around us. "I think somebody called out the Coast Guard."

I looked behind us and saw that there were several search boats nearby, but it was Seth's boat that was closest.

He'd apparently seen the safety marker buoy.

"Seth called for help," I told her as the boat approached.

"Mom's going to be upset," Wren said.

"Of course she's going to be upset," I said shortly. "She's your mother."

Seth stopped and I swam behind Wren as we breached the short distance to the boat.

Brock reached for Wren the moment she put her foot on the ladder.

By the time I got on deck, Wren was already in her mother's arms.

It almost killed me when I saw that Emma was sobbing as she held our daughter tightly.

"You scared me," Emma said tearfully to Wren as she hugged her.

"I'm fine, Mom," Emma said as she hugged her mother back. "The current wasn't bad, but I got tangled up in some rope. Dad found me and got me loose."

I watched as Emma wrapped her daughter's wet body in a towel and handed her some water.

Brock and Seth hugged Wren before Seth went to send a radio message to the Coast Guard to let them know that my daughter was safe.

Emma turned and suddenly threw herself into my arms. "I was worried about you, too," she told me, her voice trembling with relief.

"I'm wet," I told her, but held her against me anyway.

"I don't care," she said as she hugged me tighter. "You went after our daughter and made sure she was safe."

"She's my daughter, too," I reminded her gruffly.

Emma pulled back and smiled at me. "I know. What happened down there? Brock and I noticed that the winds were starting to pick up, but we really weren't worried about currents until we saw Seth."

"It wasn't horrible," I admitted. "But it was enough to take Wren from my side. She did get tangled in some rope, and she was struggling. I never should have taken her down there."

Emma stepped back and swiped the tears from her face. "This wasn't your fault, Colin. It's the first time anything weird has happened since the day she started diving."

"Dad said I can't dive anymore," Wren said to her mother as she moved beside her. "He's being completely irrational."

"I don't care," I said grumpily. "There's absolutely no reason to put you at risk by going back underwater."

"I'm going to be a marine scientist. I can't stop diving," Wren said reasonably.

"You are being a little irrational," Brock pointed out. "Diving is relatively safe. It's just as safe as any other sport as long as you take all of the necessary precautions."

"No sports of any kind," I said hoarsely. "Nothing that's going to put my daughter at risk. I think that incident just took ten years off my life."

I saw Brock and Seth exchange surprised glances before Seth moved forward in the boat.

"I'll get us back to shore," Seth said carefully.

"We'll discuss this later," Emma said firmly. "This incident scared everyone, Wren. We'll talk about it after everyone has a chance to calm down."

Wren nodded reluctantly and went to sit in one of the loungers as the boat sped up.

Emma gripped the railing, and I stood behind her and wrapped an arm around her waist.

It was almost impossible to talk to her about anything over the sound of the boat's engine without raising my voice more than I wanted to at the moment.

It was hard to tell if she was angry, but she probably had a right to be.

I'd definitely overstepped by telling Wren she couldn't dive anymore without speaking with Emma about it first.

She was her mother.

Christ! How did anybody live through this whole parenting thing?

Emma had probably been through similar scares during Wren's childhood and she wasn't flipping out and telling her daughter she couldn't do anything that was remotely dangerous again.

I knew I'd completely lost it with Wren, and nothing that had happened was *her* fault.

Yeah, she'd struggled with the rope, but she hadn't gone into a diver panic.

She'd just been confused, which was perfectly normal considering the circumstances.

I *was* being unreasonable, but how did a parent protect their kid without overreacting?

Seeing Wren in trouble had terrified the hell out of me.

I was probably more rational than most people, but I was losing my shit about protecting my child.

Emma suddenly reached back and put her hand over mine on the railing.

She squeezed my fingers in a comforting gesture, and my tense muscles started to relax a little.

She was trying to comfort *me* even though I'd crossed a line with her today.

Fucking hell!

I didn't deserve it, but I'd take it and apologize to her later.

CHAPTER 29

Emma

"I lost Wren once when she was little in a big retail store," I told Colin as we shared a lounger out by the pool after Wren had gone to bed. "One second she was right beside me, and a moment later she was gone. I panicked."

Colin had been brooding all evening about how he'd handled the situation with Wren earlier, and it needed to stop.

He'd sat our daughter down after dinner and explained that he'd reacted that way because he'd been incredibly worried about her.

She'd given him a hug after that discussion was over and asked if he'd be okay with her diving again in the future.

He'd given her a noncommittal "we'll see" answer.

"You must have found her," he commented.

"I did," I confirmed. "It didn't really take long. She'd wandered into another aisle, but I spent those moments completely freaked out. After I found her I swore I'd never take my daughter to a crowded place ever again. I lamented about what a horrible mother I was for days afterward. I also scolded my daughter more than I should have because she scared the crap out of me."

He turned his head to look at me. "What are you trying to say?"

I sighed. "I'm trying to make you understand that no parent is perfect. I've made plenty of mistakes, but Wren is a good kid anyway. You're going to have to let her dive again."

"Can you really do that after what happened?" Colin asked.

"Yes."

"Why?"

"Because I know it's relatively safe," I said calmly. "I was scared, too, but it's not the first time my daughter has worried me over the years. Every illness and injury she's had scared me, but you kind of get used to worrying about your child. You learn to protect them as much as you can, but you know you can't prevent everything that happens. You'd have to put your kid in a bubble for that, and that's not good for their development."

"Why does it have to be scuba diving?" Colin said in a disgruntled tone.

"It's the only thing she's ever begged me to do. It's the only sport she's ever been interested in. She wants to be a marine biologist with an advanced degree so she can do research. If she's going to be diving for a living in the future, I'd rather she have as much exposure and as much experience as possible from the beginning."

"Fuck!" he cursed. "I guess that's true."

"She grew up here, Colin," I said reasonably. "She's been in Lake Michigan since she was old enough to play in the shallows. She'd like to experience some ocean diving. She'll need you to guide her for that. Wren will be fifteen in two years, and she'll be able to dive independently."

"Not happening," he said stoically. "I'll be there for every single dive as long as she's underage."

I nodded. "I don't think I'd be able to let her go without parental supervision even when she meets the age requirements. She's always going to need a dive buddy, and I'd prefer that it's one of her parents until she's an adult."

I should probably remind him that he wasn't always going to be here when Wren wanted to dive, but I didn't.

He'd probably had enough parental trauma for one day.

I knew Colin would eventually see sense once he got over all of that initial fear of seeing his daughter in a bad situation.

I'd been exactly where he was right now many times in the past.

"How in the hell did you manage to live through the first thirteen years of her life?" Colin asked unhappily.

"It was hard when she was a baby and a toddler," I confessed. "I worried about everything. But I had to eventually send her to school. Letting go is always hard."

"I was pretty harsh with her today, Emma," he shared. "Nothing that happened was her fault. I let my fear get the better of me. I've never done that before."

"Get used to it," I teased. "Wren just lets it roll off her back because she understands that our fear is a product of love. Did she seem upset to you when she went to bed?"

"No," Colin mused. "But she had a right to be upset. I know I can't just stroll into her life and tell her what to do. But it's damn hard to fight the urge to protect her."

I knew he was struggling, and I hated that for him.

He was fighting the fatherly instinct to protect his daughter while trying not to come on too strong with Wren because he hadn't been around for her during the last thirteen years.

"I don't really need to tell her what to do anymore, Colin. She has a good head on her shoulders. She does all of her chores without me needing to remind her. For the most part, I let her reason things out herself because she's capable of doing it. She just needs some guidance sometimes. You'll figure that out after she's been in your life for a while."

"I hope so," he grumbled. "Right now I'd like to put her in that bubble and make sure that she never gets hurt."

I smiled. "You know that's not realistic. We learn from our mistakes and getting hurt once in a while."

"Yeah, well, it seems that my rational mind has fled my body since I met my daughter," he rumbled.

"I wish I could tell you that it gets easier," I told him. "It really doesn't, but you'll learn to tolerate those emotions a lot better because you want what's best for your child."

"I'll talk to her tomorrow," he promised. "I know I can't keep her from something she loves because of my own irrational fears. I overreacted."

"I know," I said softly. "Been there and done it myself more times than I can count."

"Have I told you what an incredible woman you are, Em?" he asked huskily.

I laughed. "Because I freak out over my daughter sometimes?"

He shook his head. "Because you've been an incredible mother to our daughter. You always seem to know exactly what to say to Wren."

"It's taken me thirteen years of practice to get to this point," I reminded him. "Be patient with yourself, Colin."

"I know that I can never be the parent you've been to her," he said thoughtfully. "I just want to be there for you and Wren in the future. I want to make up for all of the times when I wasn't there for you."

I shook my head slowly. "You don't need to make up for the past. You didn't know about Wren. We just want you to be here now."

"I'll be here whenever you need me," he confirmed. "You know I'm going back to California on Sunday, but I'll probably be here more than you'd like. It's going to feel like an eternity before you and Wren get to California for the holidays."

We'd already agreed to spend the holidays together in California.

I wanted to remind him that the holidays weren't that far away, but it was going to seem like forever to me, too.

It had been a magical summer, but I knew it was time for both of us to get back to the real world.

I had a daughter who was starting high school, and Wren had to be my priority.

I had to get her back into her usual routine.

It wasn't going to be easy for Wren to be without her father after spending time with him, so I was going to have to be strong.

I wasn't going to be able to just wallow in my misery and loneliness once Colin had returned to his home in California.

We'd argued about him paying regular child support, but I'd lost that battle.

He wanted to do his fair share, so I'd put that money into an account for Wren for her future needs once she became an adult.

He *was* a father who had never known about his daughter, and I couldn't stop him from doing what he felt was his responsibility.

If I was in his position, I'd probably feel the same way.

He was a man who needed to contribute somehow, and it would kill him not to feel like he was providing for his daughter.

I'd be lying to myself if I tried to pretend like I didn't want a future with Colin.

I wanted that so badly that my heart ached to be with him.

But it was way too early to talk about that.

He'd only been back in my life for a short amount of time.

I loved him and that was never going to change, but I wasn't sure he felt the same way.

I knew he cared about me and Wren.

I knew he wanted our relationship to continue in the future.

But we'd never talked about being together for the rest of our lives, and logically, it didn't really make sense to talk about that at this point in our relationship.

I'd probably figure out a way to move to California if I knew that was what he wanted, but he still hadn't said a word about Wren and me moving closer to him.

"It's not Sunday yet," I reminded him as I crawled on top of him and looked down at the man I was going to miss like crazy.

He wrapped his arms tightly around my waist. "It's only a few days away," he answered.

My heart squeezed so hard inside my chest that I felt like it was going to explode.

I knew that, but I wanted to forget that he was leaving until I had to be without him again.

"Then I guess we need to make the next few nights count," I told him as I moved my body sensually on top of his. "Take me to bed, Colin."

He framed my face with his hands and caught my gaze.

Our eyes locked, and I wasn't quite sure how long we stayed like that, but I was sure that he could see the longing in my eyes.

"Emma," he said in a solemn tone. "I—"

I cut him off by dropping my lips to his.

I didn't want to talk about him leaving again.

I didn't want to think about how I'd feel when he wasn't with me anymore.

I was going to spend a lot of lonely nights without Colin but tonight wasn't one of those nights.

Right now, I was his and he was mine.

I'd spent the last fourteen years missing him.

"Just make love to me," I whispered after the tender embrace had ended.

There were nights when we made love, and there were nights when sex with Colin was primal and carnal.

I needed all of the tenderness and affection that he could give me along with the sexual satisfaction tonight.

He slapped me on the ass when I started to move my hips against his rampant erection.

"Fuck!" he said on strangled groan. "I think you're always going to make me completely insane, woman."

God, I hoped so.

He got the two of us out of the lounger, picked me up, and carried me into his bedroom.

We spent the rest of the night completely forgetting that anything existed except for the two of us and the passion between us.

CHAPTER 30

Marshall

"Earth to Marshall," Wyatt said a few weeks later while we were in the conference room of the Last Hope headquarters. "Did you hear what I said?"

"Sorry," I muttered as I looked up from the file I was supposed to be studying. "I guess I lost my focus."

In reality, I'd just been staring at the words on paper.

I'd been completely worthless since the day I'd said goodbye to my woman and my child.

Emma and I spoke on the phone twice a day.

Once in the morning, and again in the evening after Wren went to bed.

I talked to Wren every day after school.

It wasn't enough.

There wasn't a single moment of the day when I didn't want to actually be there with them in person.

Every day was pure hell for me right now.

"Your focus has been nonexistent since the moment you got back from Michigan," Wyatt said drily. "Don't you think it's time for you to admit that you're not functioning well without Emma?"

"Do you think I don't know that?" I growled as I slammed my fist on the table. "What am I supposed to do about that?"

Wyatt lifted a brow. "You could start by admitting that you love her and that you want to be in the same place with her."

"I do love her," I grumbled. "I probably always have."

I'd almost told her that when I was in Michigan when we were sharing a lounger by the pool a few days before I'd left.

She'd kissed me before I could get those words out of my mouth.

Later, my rational mind had prevailed.

What if she didn't feel the same way?

We hadn't really been together for long.

What if those weren't words that she wanted to hear yet?

I'd convinced myself that she needed more time, and that I'd have to patient.

"I think it would help if you just told her," Wyatt observed.

"And then what?" I said gruffly.

He shrugged. "And then you figure it out. You're an intelligent guy. If you want to be with Emma and Wren, you find a way to make it happen. It's not like you *can't* live in Cherry Cove if you want to. There are five other guys who can run the actual missions for Last Hope. You can do all of the planning and research remotely."

"You guys would do that?" I asked hesitantly.

"You know we would," Wyatt answered. "We're all here for the operations anyway. We're all perfectly capable of running the rescues. You've given up your entire life for Last Hope, Marshall. I think it's time for you to do what makes *you* happy."

"It used to be my priority," I admitted. "But my priorities have changed."

He nodded. "I get that. Shelby and my unborn child are my priorities. That doesn't mean that I don't care about Last Hope, but I'd give it up for my wife and my child if necessary."

Hell, I'd give up anything for Emma and Wren, too.

Last Hope had been my entire life until I'd realized that there were things in my life that were more important than the organization I'd poured myself into for years.

Our mission here meant a lot to me, but not as much as my woman and my child.

"What if Emma doesn't want me to intrude on her life in Cherry Cove?" I asked Wyatt.

"I find that highly unlikely," Wyatt replied. "Brock mentioned that Emma hasn't been herself since you left. I think she's missing you as much as you're missing her. I guess you're just going to have to ask her."

He was right.

All of this was complete bullshit.

I loved Emma, and I was going to have to take that risk.

I'd copped out after my first attempt at telling her how I felt.

I'd made excuses, but in reality, I'd probably been afraid that she wasn't going to be able to say those words back to me yet.

"Get out of your own head, Marshall," Wyatt added. "That rational brain of yours is going to ruin something you've wanted for a long time if you don't. Love isn't always rational. It took me a long time to realize that. I finally had no choice but to pull my head out of my ass, but you already know that."

I slowly nodded.

I'd seen every one of my partners go through their own personal hell before they'd found their own happiness.

I'd never understood why anyone would want to go through that for a woman.

But I understood it *now*.

Emma wasn't just *any* woman.

She was *my* woman.

If I would have pulled my head out of my ass fourteen years ago, I would have realized that a long time ago.

"I need to go back to Michigan and talk to her about this in person," I told Wyatt.

I wasn't going to tell her that I loved her for the first time on the damn phone.

He grinned at me and looked at his watch. "No need. Emma will be landing here in two hours."

I gaped at him. "How is that possible?"

"Shelby was worried about you. She said your brain was total shit and that you weren't yourself. She called Emma and asked her to come because you needed her. Wren is staying with Brock for the next week. You have a week to convince Emma that the two of you need to be together. Don't fuck it up, Marshall. You *do* need her."

It took a moment for that information to sink into my brain.

Emma was coming *here*?

In two hours?

"I'll pick her up at the airport," I sputtered, my heart thundering in my ears.

Wyatt shook his head. "No need for that, either. Shelby is taking a limo herself to get Emma. I think she wants a little time for some girl talk. She'll drop her off at your place. I suggest you use the next few hours to find a ring so you can ask Emma to marry you. That is what you want, right?"

"It's exactly what I want, but—"

"For once in your life stop thinking, Marshall," Wyatt said firmly. "Go with your gut and your heart. Go after what you want and screw everything else. For what it's worth, I don't think Emma is going to say *no*. She literally dropped everything to get here to California because she thought you needed her. Shelby made sure that she knew that you weren't physically hurt."

"What did Shelby tell her?" I asked.

Wyatt shrugged. "I'm not exactly sure, but whatever she said got Emma on my jet."

"I should probably be pissed off about this," I grumbled.

"But you're not because you want to see Emma," Wyatt countered. "You have friends here who care about you, Marshall. You know how much Shelby cares. It bothered her to see you this unhappy. It unsettles all of us. Marry Emma for fuck's sake and go back to being your normal asshole self again."

I grinned at Wyatt. "I'll never be quite the same guy."

Hell, I hadn't been the same guy since the moment I'd seen Emma again.

"I can live with that as long as your brain finds its way back into your head."

I'd never really stopped to appreciate the people who were important in my life here in California.

Granted, I wasn't a people person, and I'd never really hung out with my billionaire partners on a regular basis, but they *were* important in my life.

"I'm not good at thanking anyone for anything," I said hesitantly.

Wyatt let out an exasperated breath. "We're your friends, Marshall. I've lost track of how many times you've helped all of us and actually saved our asses when we needed your help. In my mind, whatever we can do for you is pathetically small in exchange for all of the things you've done for us for years."

"It's a big deal to me," I told him honestly.

My friends were helping me pull my head out of my ass and getting Emma to California so I could fix this situation.

That meant a lot to me.

"Then we'll have a beer when this is over and you can thank us when we're together. We'll all tell you that thanks are never needed. Now get out of here. I think you have things you need to do."

I got to my feet. "I think I should let Emma pick out her own ring."

I was definitely asking her to marry me, but if by some miracle she did say *yes*, I wanted Emma to have something she loved on her finger.

Wyatt grimaced. "She'll pick out something small and barely noticeable."

I hadn't thought about that.

Knowing Emma, she'd be worried about keeping the ring within some kind of budget because that was the way she'd always lived.

"She's always lived on a budget because she was raising Wren by herself," I pondered. "You're right. I'll stop by the jewelry store on the way home."

I knew what Emma liked in antique jewelry, but she was getting a ring that was all hers and that had never been worn by anyone else this time.

"Call me when you get all of this resolved," Wyatt called out as I headed toward the door.

"You'll be the first one to know," I called back.

The fact that Emma was on her way to California from Michigan hadn't quite sunk in for me yet, but I needed to get my ass moving and get some things done.

I'd realized that I'd made a huge mistake by leaving Michigan in the first place without letting Emma know exactly how I felt.

I should have just taken my chances and said the words I'd wanted to say before I'd left the state.

What in the hell had I been thinking?

Emma had been a gift that had been given to me for the second time in my life, and I'd left again without telling her how I felt.

I knew exactly why I'd done it.

I hadn't wanted to leave myself wide open to getting my heart broken if she didn't feel the same way I did.

I'd made every excuse possible not to put myself in that position.

Fuck that!

I'd spent most of my life doing what I thought was rational, and that definitely hadn't made me happy.

I was going to take my one shot at happiness and forget about the possible consequences.

It was something I should have done fourteen fucking years ago, and I was tired of living with regrets.

CHAPTER 31

Emma

I was still worrying about Colin as I stood in front of the door of his home in California.

Shelby had made it clear that there was nothing physically wrong with him, but she'd said he wasn't focusing on anything and that he wasn't the same man he'd been when he'd left California for Michigan.

That worried me.

Colin was the most focused and self-disciplined guy I'd ever known.

She'd also mentioned that he just seemed sad, and that had killed me.

I'd wanted to see him in person, and Shelby had made that happen in a heartbeat for me.

I liked Shelby.

She was a sweet woman, and it was clear that she really cared about Colin.

She hadn't gone into a lot of detail about him except for the fact that he wasn't functioning normally.

That was all I'd really needed to hear.

If he really needed me, I was here for him.

I didn't intend to be a long-distance girlfriend who only wanted to hear about pleasant things.

He'd never mentioned anything about his lack of focus or his issues on the phone with me, but we *were* going to talk about it in person.

Obviously, something bad had happened since he'd returned to California.

He was hiding something that was eating him alive, and I was going to find out *exactly* what was up with him.

What if his altered mental status was happening because of some kind of medical condition?

Maybe there were no physical symptoms that he was willing to tell anyone about, but he *might* be sick.

That thought had been plaguing me since Shelby had first called me.

I hadn't told Wren that I thought her dad might be ill. I'd just told her that I really wanted to talk to Colin in person. She'd very happily agreed to stay with Brock for as long as I wanted to stay in California.

I wouldn't stay long.

I just wanted to assure myself that nothing was wrong with Colin.

I didn't think that Shelby was the type of woman who got worried about nothing, and Colin obviously wasn't going to share anything with me long distance that might get me worried.

I looked around after I rang the doorbell.

Colin's house was large, and Shelby had explained that it was an affluent neighborhood.

The large front yard was meticulously kept, which didn't surprise me.

I was willing to bet that the back yard was just as nice as the front.

Shelby had told me that Colin was expecting me, but I was still surprised by how quickly the front door flew open.

I didn't have a chance to say a word as Colin pulled me inside, slammed the front door closed, and pinned me to the wall beside the door.

"Emma," he growled. "Fuck! I missed you."

I didn't get a chance to tell him that I'd missed him just as much.

His mouth came down on mine with a ferocity that had my body flooding with desire in a nanosecond.

God, I'd missed him, too.

So. Damn. Much.

I'd been fighting to keep my spirits up for Wren's sake, but nothing had been quite right since Colin had left Cherry Cove.

My body had missed him.

My heart had missed him.

And the pain had been so torturous that I'd felt it deep in my soul.

"Colin," I gasped when he'd finally finished devouring my mouth.

"We'll talk later," he said huskily as he nipped at the sensitive skin at my neck.

"Later," I said on a long sigh as he reached for the button of my jeans.

Nothing mattered at the moment except the burning desire to be together.

Clothing flew everywhere frantically until we were both naked.

"I've been thinking about you every damn second of every day since I got back to California," he said in a low, dangerous baritone.

I let out a needy whimper as he pressed me against the wall and slid a hand down my body.

My breath caught as he stroked his possessive fingers inside the wet folds of my pussy.

One touch.

One bold stroke over my clit.

And I was ready to lose my mind.

Colin was the only man who could do this to my body, and I just didn't care that I was this vulnerable to him.

I trusted him.

"You're wet for me, Em," he rasped as he stroked over my clit in a rhythmic motion.

"Yes," I admitted readily, my whole body vibrating with need.

"Come for me," he demanded. "Once I get my cock inside you, it's not going to last long."

My head fell back against the wall with a loud *thud*.

There was no way that I *wasn't* going to come.

My climax was already unfurling inside my belly.

Maybe it had only been a few weeks, but it felt like it had been forever since this man had touched me.

He gave me the pressure and stimulation I needed and slammed his mouth down on mine.

His kiss was rough, hot, hungry and carnal, and I moaned against his lips as my body responded to his demands.

When he finally let me come up for air, my orgasm was rolling over me so powerfully that I screamed, "Colin!"

I closed my eyes, but I could still feel him watching me as I found my release.

He didn't rush that process.

In fact, he stroked me until he'd rung every ounce of pleasure from me that he could get.

"Watching you come is the sexiest thing I've ever seen," he grunted as he lifted me by the ass and urged my legs around his waist.

"Fuck me!" I panted as I gripped his shoulders.

I wanted Colin to fill the emptiness inside me because he was the only one who could.

My heart was pounding in anticipation, and I felt like I couldn't wait another second to feel the two of us intimately connected.

He didn't make me wait.

Colin gripped my ass hard and surged inside me.

My breath caught as he buried himself to his balls.

There was nothing gentle about this coupling, but it was exactly what I needed at the moment.

Just him.

Just us.

Just the frenzied emotion that ricocheted through my entire body as he started to move.

I relished every powerful, desperate thrust of his cock, my short nails digging into the skin of his back because the pleasure was so intense.

"You're mine, Emma!" he growled, his breath hot and heavy on my neck. "You always have been and always will be."

This man was claiming me, and there was nothing sexier than that because I wanted to be his.

"Yes!" I panted.

I'd belonged to Colin from the moment he'd helped me up in Virginia Beach after plowing me over on the sidewalk.

I'd felt it instantly.

It had just taken a while for my brain to catch up to my heart.

"I love you," I panted, my emotions all over the place.

"Fucking hell!" he said in a hoarse voice. "I love you, too, Em."

I hadn't meant to say those words, but I hadn't been able to hold them inside me any longer.

I was hopelessly, ridiculously, utterly in love with Colin Marshall, and that was never going to change.

His pace increased, and he fucked me like a man possessed.

I savored the ferocity of every powerful surge.

Colin was *mine*.

I felt it in every cell of my body.

When he slid a hand between our bodies and stroked my clit, I knew he was on the edge.

Every ragged breath.

Every sensual slide of damp skin as we moved together.

Every single touch made me completely insane.

That was when I completely let go and flew over the edge.

"Colin," I screamed loudly, my heart beating so hard that it felt like it was about to explode.

"Emma," he groaned as the spasms from my climax started to milk his cock.

The two of us got completely lost in our pleasure.

I wasn't sure how long it lasted.

I lost track of everything except for the man who was holding me like he was never going to let go.

My head fell limply to his shoulder in the aftermath, and there wasn't a sound in the room except for our frantic breaths as we held tightly to each other.

At some point, he reached down and grabbed something out of the pocket of his jeans before he lifted me up and started carrying me to another room.

CHAPTER 32

Emma

Colin took us to what I assumed was the living room, dropped me gently on the sofa, and wrapped our nude bodies in a blanket from the back of the couch after he'd come down beside me.

"I'm not even going to ask the question. You're going to marry me and put me out of my misery. If you don't, it's going to kill me," he said grumpily as he held up a box and opened it.

I gasped as he unceremoniously slid a beautiful diamond ring onto the ring finger of my left hand.

The ring was breathtaking, a gorgeous engagement ring fashioned in an art deco style with an enormous diamond in the center.

"Colin?" I questioned breathlessly.

He shook his head. "You love me. I love you. We should have been together a long time ago, Em. We're getting married."

I had to bite my lip to keep from smiling.

His proposal had been so typically Colin.

When he decided he was going to do something, he did it without a lot of fuss or fanfare.

"Do I have a say in this?" I teased.

"No," he said flatly. "Only if you really don't want the same thing. You said that you love me. I should have said it first back in Michigan, but I was worried that you didn't feel the same way."

"I do love you," I said hesitantly. "But what about our little geography problem? And I came here because I was worried about you. Are you sick? Shelby says that you aren't yourself right now."

He'd taken me by surprise, but my heart was enthusiastically agreeing with his proposition.

I wanted to marry Colin.

I wanted to be with him more than anything else in the world.

But we still had the same issues.

"There's nothing wrong with me that you marrying me won't cure," he said huskily as he pulled me into his lap. "My heart isn't into anything I'm doing here right now. All I can think about is how stupid it was for me to leave the woman I loved and my daughter back in Cherry Cove. I'll move to Michigan, Emma. I've already spoken to my partners, and they're willing to do the missions from headquarters. I can sell my place here and get us a bigger place there."

Wait! What?

My heart flipped over inside my chest.

Was he really saying that he was willing to give up his entire life here to live in Michigan?

Last Hope had been everything to him for years.

I leaned back so I could see his face.

His eyes were dead serious.

He *was* going to give everything up for me and for Wren.

Tears filled my eyes, and my heart squeezed *hard* inside my chest.

He cared about us *that* much.

He loved us *that* much.

I stroked his jaw as tears plopped onto my cheeks. "You can't just give up everything you care about here."

"I can," he said nonchalantly as he gently swiped a tear from my face. "Nothing here comes close to the way I love you and my daughter. I can't be happy here without you. Shelby was right. I'm not myself here anymore because you're in Michigan and I'm here in California."

For him, it was just that simple.

For me, it was complicated.

Because I loved him, I didn't want him to give up Last Hope for me.

"You've never asked me if I'd be willing to move to California," I mused. "It would be a better environment for Wren. Better schools with advanced programs for her. She has friends here, and my mom is here."

"I can't just ask you to uproot your entire life in Michigan," he grumbled. "What if I had asked?"

I sighed. "I would have wanted to do it. I thought about moving after my mother moved here. Wren and I miss her. I knew there would be more opportunities for Wren's education, and the weather is nice in Southern California year-round. Money was always a deciding factor for me. It's expensive to live here, and I'm a single mother."

"What if money wasn't an issue and I asked you to move here?" he asked.

"Then I'd move in a heartbeat," I confessed. "Wren and I would have missed our friends in Michigan, but we'd have you and my mom here. I can make new friends and see the old ones when I can. Wren is already complaining about missing California."

"She just started school," he argued.

I rolled my eyes. "Are you really worried that she'll fall behind from the move?"

His arm tightened around my waist. "Will you marry me and move here?" he asked hesitantly.

I laughed as I touched the beautiful ring on my finger. "You're finally going to ask?"

"I'm asking," he confirmed.

There was a vulnerability in his tone that touched my heart.

I swallowed the lump in my throat and nodded. "I think we'd all be happier here."

"If you marry me and move here, I'll make damn sure that you never regret it," he stated solemnly.

"I know I'll never regret it," I said as I happily snuggled up against him. "We'll be together."

"We should have been together years ago," he griped. "If I'd made it back to you before you left Virginia Beach, I never would have let you go."

"It's a miracle that we're actually getting a second chance," I reminded him.

I didn't want to think about what our life could have been like had things gone differently.

I was just grateful that Colin was here with me *now*.

"I'm not complaining about that," he assured me. "I guess I just want you to know that I'm not stupid enough to do the same thing twice. I'm always going to hold onto what should have been ours years ago. When are you going to marry me?"

"It's going to take a while to plan a wedding, put my place up for sale, and get us moved here," I mused. "I need to get Wren enrolled in school here."

"I'll take care of the details here," Colin offered. "Put your house up for sale and I'll hire some movers. I'll admit that I'm impatient with this whole situation, Em. I want you and Wren here with me."

I didn't really want to wait, either.

I'd spent years missing Colin, and I didn't want to waste any more time missing him when I didn't have to do it.

I wanted him.

Wren wanted to be with her father.

My heart wasn't in Michigan anymore.

It was here in California with Colin.

"I'll put my place up for sale when I get back to Michigan," I told him. "We can wait a little longer, right?"

"Probably not," he said grumpily. "If you wait too long I'll be back in Cherry Cove to visit. How long can you stay here?"

My heart soared because I definitely wasn't going to argue about a visit while we had to be apart. "Not long," I admitted. "Brock will spoil the crap out of our daughter while I'm gone. He gives her whatever she wants. I only came to see if there was something wrong with you. I was worried."

"Nothing is wrong with me except that I was regretting being an asshole and leaving you," he assured me. "I should have put a damn ring on your finger when I was in Cherry Cove. I just wasn't sure if you wanted to commit to a future together."

"I wanted it," I answered. "I just wasn't sure what you wanted. All of this happened so fast."

"Not that fast," he countered. "It's been fourteen years, Emma. I think I knew what I wanted back in Virginia Beach, but I had nothing to offer you. I'd spent my life dedicated to service in the US Navy. I was gone most of the time, and my mind was always on a mission. I thought that you deserved a guy a lot better than me."

Frustrated, I moved until I was straddling Colin and staring into his beautiful gray eyes. "You were completely focused on me in Virginia Beach. There never was and never will be another man for me."

He grinned back at me, and my heart melted.

"You were one hell of a distraction," he replied. "You still are."

"I love you," I whispered as I fell into his intense gaze.

"I love you, too, Em," he said roughly. "There's never been another woman for me, either."

"I know you're not a big believer in fate," I answered. "But I am. I think fate threw me the man I needed after being completely destroyed by one who wasn't the guy for me. I'll always be grateful for that. You were always good to me and good for me, whether you realize that or not."

There was no better man on the planet for me, and I wanted him to know that.

"I'll always be good to you, Emma," he promised. "It's too damn late to worry about whether or not I'm good enough for you. You're stuck with me."

I smiled down at him. "I want to be stuck with you. I love my ring, but the diamond is enormous."

I loved it, but I knew it had been costly, and as a single mom, I'd always worried about money.

It was going to be an adjustment for me not to think about finances and raising a child on my own all the time.

He shrugged. "You're going to marry me, and I want every guy out there to know you're already mine."

I snorted. "You say that like every guy is going to want me."

I was forty-six, plump, and not the woman of every man's dreams. But…when I was with Colin, I *did* feel like the woman of *his* dreams. He'd probably never know how amazing it was to feel that way.

"It doesn't matter if they want you," he said. "You're already mine. Now tell me when we're going to make that official."

"As soon as possible?" I suggested.

He flipped us until his body was covering mine on the sofa. "Not good enough, Emma. I'm getting that date before you go back to Michigan."

I wrapped my arms around his neck and wriggled my hips against him. "Then we have a little time to figure it out."

"Emma," he said in a warning voice.

My heart stuttered as I realized that he was as hard as a rock.

"Make love to me, Colin. We'll figure everything out. I need you. I just need to be with you right now."

"How am I supposed to argue about that?" he asked gruffly.

"You're not supposed to," I said in a seductive voice.

"Hell, you make me completely insane," he said in a voice that told me he didn't care if he became a lunatic.

As soon his lips met mine, neither of us cared about anything else for quite some time.

EPILOGUE

Marshall
A Few Months Later...

"I can't believe we're married now," Emma said with a happy sigh as I held her in my arms on the dance floor of our wedding reception.

I usually wasn't a dancing kind of guy, but I wasn't going to miss the opportunity to hold my bride on our wedding day.

So, I was dancing, and Emma wasn't complaining about my lack of dance skills or the way I was limping through the dance.

Honestly, I didn't really know what other people thought anymore.

She didn't care about my lack of skills or finesse on the dance floor, and that was all that really mattered to me.

Yeah, we *were* finally fucking married, and it had been the longest few months of my life.

I'd quickly arranged the details to get Emma and my daughter to California, and I'd gotten that accomplished in less than a month.

It hadn't taken long for Emma to become fast friends with my partners' wives, and Wren had continued on with her friendships here like she'd never left them.

My daughter professed that she loved her new school, and she spent as much time with her grandmother and her friends as she possibly could.

Emma and I had visited her mom soon after I'd put a ring on Emma's finger.

Okay, I'd been a little nervous about meeting her mom.

I *had* been the man who had knocked her daughter up and left her alone to raise our child.

Even though she'd known that I'd never known about Wren, it would have still been easy for her to resent me for not being there for her daughter and my child anyway.

I hated it myself, so I wouldn't have blamed her if she had resented my absence during some of those difficult times for her daughter.

Luckily, her mother had accepted me easily and enthusiastically, without a single hint of displeasure that I'd just shown up out of the blue.

We'd gotten even closer since that initial meeting.

Emma was a lot like her mother, which made her mom a very easy woman to like.

Once Emma and Wren had physically moved, all of the other details had gotten wrapped up quickly.

I'd solved the problem of putting Emma's house up for sale by paying it off and giving it to Emma as an early wedding gift.

She and Wren would miss the people they cared about in Michigan, so I thought I'd remedy that by spending time in Michigan when we could.

Emma had started planning the wedding as soon as she'd moved to California, but it couldn't happen fast enough for me.

The guest list had stayed extremely small, thank God.

Wren, Emma's mother, Sara, my partners, their wives, and the Michigan team were all here at the reception, along with a few other people that we'd wanted to share this special day with us.

Sara had been Emma's maid of honor, and Wyatt had stood up for me in our simple, short, but meaningful wedding ceremony.

I couldn't say that I was actually enjoying my time in a tuxedo, but seeing Emma in her ivory wedding gown had made up for any discomfort I was feeling.

Emma had my ring on her finger and my last name now, and that was the best part of this entire day for me.

I had to admit that I'd gotten a little choked up when Wren had asked me if she could take my last name, too.

Wren would be a Marshall soon because she really *wanted* to be.

My entire life had changed in a very short period of time, and I felt like the luckiest bastard on the planet today.

"We're married," I confirmed. "It's too late for second thoughts now."

Emma shook her head. "No second thoughts. I like it here, and I love *you*. Your house is actually starting to look like a home now."

Fuck! I'd probably never get used to hearing Emma tell me that she loved me, and I knew I'd never take the love and trust Emma had given me for granted.

I'd lived without that for so damn long that it was always going to feel like a miracle to me.

"It's *our* home," I reminded her. "You'll probably miss your friends."

Our place *was* starting to look like a real home.

Emma was starting to put some personality and warmth into the home by adding a lot of pictures and some color into the utilitarian house.

Yeah, there was clutter that I happily put away when necessary, but I had a wife and kid now.

Our home actually looked like a *family* lived there now, and I wouldn't ever want to go back to the way it used to be.

I could feel the love and warmth in the home the minute I walked through the door every day.

For a guy who had lived a solitary, lonely life for so many years it was the best feeling in the world.

Granted, I'd never known what I was missing when I was alone, but now that I knew how happy I could be, I was never going back to the miserable asshole I'd been my entire life.

"I'll miss them," she confirmed. "They were always a huge part of my life because I had no family in Michigan after Mom left. I'd like to think they'll all end up as happy as I am right now. I think there's someone out there for all of them. The guys swear they'll never get married, but I think they just need to meet the right women. They're going to have to meet someone who is more important to them than Last Hope and the secrecy and privacy of their lives. They need someone they can trust."

I thought about that for a moment. "Not that long ago, I would have said that will probably never happen. But if it happened to me at my age, it can definitely happen for them. I thought my partners would be single forever, but all of them found the right woman."

Emma sighed. "It's going to take some females who can see through their bullshit."

"Like you saw through mine," I said drily.

Hell, I was probably the coldest, unemotional asshole in Last Hope.

If I could end up with a woman like Emma, it could happen for any of the other guys.

Emma pulled back a little and smiled at me. "I always could," she told me. "I'm not sure why most people can't see through that big, bad, SEAL commander crap. You have an amazing heart underneath that façade."

"I'd prefer that everyone else still sees me as a rational leader," I told her.

Wyatt was the only one who had ever really seen me lose my shit, and I wanted to keep it that way.

"I'll never tell," she teased. "The people who know you the best already know the truth. You're a good man, Colin Marshall. The people who follow your orders at Last Hope without question already know that. It's a volunteer organization. If they didn't believe in you, they wouldn't be there."

"You don't exactly follow my orders without question," I grumbled.

"You don't need another faithful follower," she joked. "You need a woman who loves you and isn't afraid to question you when necessary."

She was probably right.

I needed someone to call me out occasionally because very few people did.

Her occasional stubbornness made me crazy at times, but it was also one of the many reasons I loved her.

Loving my wife so damn much was a vulnerability for me, and that was something I'd avoided all of my life.

It had taken me a while to realize that sometimes having a few vulnerabilities was worth the risk.

I was willing to do anything to make sure that Emma and Wren stayed safe and happy, and I didn't give a shit anymore if everyone knew it.

"Are you sure you're not disappointed that we aren't having a long, romantic honeymoon?" I questioned.

We were taking a few days to go to Catalina Island, but that wasn't a real honeymoon in my mind.

"No," she said softly. "It's almost Christmas. Every day that we're together feels like a honeymoon to me, Colin. It will be our first holiday season together. I just want to be with my family."

"We're going on a real honeymoon after the holidays," I grumbled.

"We'll see," she said noncommittally.

We *were* going.

We'd had a small, intimate wedding. Emma deserved a nice honeymoon. She didn't know it yet, but that was going to be a Christmas gift from me.

Emma had always wanted a Caribbean vacation, and she was getting one after the craziness of the holidays were over.

Yes, we had a daughter to raise, and we were a family. But I always wanted Emma to know that she was a huge priority in my life.

My work and Last Hope were still important to me, but it wasn't my whole life anymore.

"We have a few days to ourselves," she said as she tightened her arms around my neck. "I've never been to Catalina Island. I know it won't be beach weather, but I'm still excited to see it with you."

I'd never been there, either, even though I'd lived close to the tourist destination for years.

"It won't be as crowded as it is during beach weather," I pointed out.

"I'm good with that," she said in a seductive voice. "I can think of other things I'd rather do than go to the beach with you."

I looked down at her, and our gazes locked.

Her gorgeous blue eyes were full of mischief, love, and adoration.

Christ! I had no idea what I'd done in my life to deserve this woman, but I'd spend the rest of my life being grateful for her and the love I thought would never happen for me.

"Such as?" I questioned hoarsely.

She smiled. "It might be cool outside, but I'm sure I can find a way to get that ripped body of yours naked, hot, and sweaty without the warm weather."

She pressed her shapely body against me a little tighter.

Fucking hell!

My dick was as hard as a pike in a heartbeat.

"You don't want to see the water?" I asked gruffly.

Her smile widened. "You made sure we have an amazing water view from the villa. I want to see *you*. I'll let you escape once in a while for food and a little sightseeing."

I grinned back at her. "I'm sure we can find food delivery."

"Good," she said with a nod. "Then we can eat naked while we look at the stunning water views."

"I think it's time to get the hell out of here," I said hoarsely.

I wanted exactly what Emma wanted.

We needed a few days to ourselves while it finally sunk in that we were now a married couple.

Emma was *mine*, and I wanted to spend as much time as possible claiming her heart, mind, body, and soul.

It had been a hectic few months, and neither of us had gotten the time together that we needed.

Emma had been busy planning the wedding and we'd tried to make sure we were there for Wren when she needed us while she was adjusting to her new life in California.

I'd also been a little preoccupied with work. Prince Nick was safe at the moment, and the situation was getting a little better for him in Lania. The king's health was improving, and I'd helped him bust one more person responsible for his assassination attempt, a high official in the government that he'd previously thought was a friend.

I wanted to believe that things would be fine in Lania in the future, but I had a gut feeling that he may still have enemies out there that were going to be outed in the future.

Change wasn't going to come easily or smoothly for a country like Lania.

But, for now, the only thing I could think about was my wife and making up for the fact that I'd spent way too much time on work lately.

It was time to get this very short honeymoon started.

She nodded eagerly. "I think we can slip out now. Kiss me first, Colin."

I looked down at her beautiful face and her radiant smile before I finally lowered my mouth to hers.

This woman.

This gorgeous, vibrant, warmhearted woman was exactly what happiness looked like for me.

After a lifetime of being alone, I wanted to savor every second of that happiness.

Emma and my daughter had turned my quiet, highly structured bachelor's life upside down, but I was gladly going to wallow in the chaos of my new life.

I made sure that my kiss told Emma everything she needed to know, and all of the things that I sometimes didn't say out loud often enough.

I was always going to cherish what we had.

I was always going to be grateful that my life had changed because she was part of it.

And I was *always* going to love her like crazy.

Maybe we'd missed our first shot at a future together, but…

By some miracle, we were together after fourteen years of separation.

I *knew* what real happiness felt like *now*, and I was going to spend the rest of my life making damn sure that Emma and I never lost each other again.

~THE END~

Please visit me at:
http://www.authorjsscott.com
http://www.facebook.com/authorjsscott

You can write to me at
jsscott_author@hotmail.com

You can also tweet
@AuthorJSScott

Please sign up for my Newsletter for updates, new releases and exclusive excerpts.

Books by J. S. Scott:

The Last Hope Series

Inevitable

Billionaire Obsession Series

The Billionaire's Obsession~Simon
Heart of the Billionaire
The Billionaire's Salvation
The Billionaire's Game
Billionaire Undone~Travis
Billionaire Unmasked~Jason
Billionaire Untamed~Tate
Billionaire Unbound~Chloe
Billionaire Undaunted~Zane
Billionaire Unknown~Blake
Billionaire Unveiled~Marcus
Billionaire Unloved~Jett
Billionaire Unwed~Zeke
Billionaire Unchallenged~Carter

J. S. SCOTT

Billionaire Unattainable~Mason
Billionaire Undercover~Hudson
Billionaire Unexpected~Jax
Billionaire Unnoticed~Cooper
Billionaire Unclaimed~Chase
Billionaire Unreachable~Wyatt
Billionaire Unexplained~Kaleb
Billionaire Unforgettable~Tanner
Billionaire Undeceived~Devon

British Billionaires Series

Tell Me You're Mine
Tell Me I'm Yours
Tell Me This Is Forever

Sinclair Series

The Billionaire's Christmas
No Ordinary Billionaire
The Forbidden Billionaire
The Billionaire's Touch
The Billionaire's Voice
The Billionaire Takes All
The Billionaire's Secret

Only A Millionaire

Accidental Billionaires

Ensnared
Entangled
Enamored
Enchanted
Endeared

Walker Brothers Series

Release
Player
Damaged

INEVITABLE

The Sentinel Demons

The Sentinel Demons: The Complete Collection
A Dangerous Bargain
A Dangerous Hunger
A Dangerous Fury
A Dangerous Demon King

The Vampire Coalition Series

The Vampire Coalition: The Complete Collection
The Rough Mating of a Vampire (Prelude)
Ethan's Mate
Rory's Mate
Nathan's Mate
Liam's Mate
Daric's Mate

Changeling Encounters Series

Changeling Encounters: The Complete Collection
Mate Of The Werewolf
The Dangers Of Adopting A Werewolf
All I Want For Christmas Is A Werewolf

The Pleasures of His Punishment

The Pleasures of His Punishment: The Complete Collection
The Billionaire Next Door
The Millionaire and the Librarian
Riding with the Cop
Secret Desires of the Counselor
In Trouble with the Boss
Rough Ride with a Cowboy
Rough Day for the Teacher
A Forfeit for a Cowboy
Just what the Doctor Ordered
Wicked Romance of a Vampire

The Curve Collection: Big Girls and Bad Boys Series

The Curve Collection: The Complete Collection
The Curve Ball
The Beast Loves Curves
Curves by Design

Writing as Lane Parker

Dearest Stalker
Dearest Protector
A Christmas Dream
A Valentine's Dream
Lost: A Mountain Man Rescue Romance

A Dark Horse Novel w/ Cali MacKay

Bound
Hacked

Taken By A Trillionaire Series

Virgin for the Trillionaire by Ruth Cardello
Virgin for the Prince by J.S. Scott
Virgin to Conquer by Melody Anne
Prince Bryan: Taken By A Trillionaire

Other Titles

Well Played w/Ruth Cardello

Printed in Dunstable, United Kingdom

73729481R00139